Amelia Ann Blanford Edwards

A Poetry-book of Elder Poets,

Consisting of Songs & Sonnets, Odes & Lyrics, Selected and....

Amelia Ann Blanford Edwards

A Poetry-book of Elder Poets,
Consisting of Songs & Sonnets, Odes & Lyrics, Selected and....

ISBN/EAN: 9783744772921

Printed in Europe, USA, Canada, Australia, Japan

Cover: Foto ©Andreas Hilbeck / pixelio.de

More available books at **www.hansebooks.com**

COLLECTION

OF

BRITISH AUTHORS

TAUCHNITZ EDITION.

VOL. 1701.

A POETRY-BOOK OF ELDER POETS

(FIRST SERIES)

SELECTED AND ARRANGED BY

AMELIA B. EDWARDS.

A POETRY-BOOK OF ELDER POETS

CONSISTING OF

SONGS & SONNETS, ODES & LYRICS

SELECTED AND ARRANGED, WITH NOTES,

FROM

THE WORKS OF THE ELDER ENGLISH POETS,

DATING FROM THE BEGINNING
OF THE FOURTEENTH CENTURY TO THE MIDDLE
OF THE EIGHTEENTH CENTURY;

BY

AMELIA B. EDWARDS.

COPYRIGHT EDITION.

LEIPZIG

BERNHARD TAUCHNITZ

1878.

TO THE READER.

THESE series—each in itself complete and separate —have been compiled expressly for the Tauchnitz Collection. The First Series consists of poems, chiefly lyrical, selected from the works of the elder English Poets, beginning with Chaucer and ending with the school of Gray and Cowper. The Second Series, conceived on the same plan, will begin with Burns and end with the younger poets of to-day. Taken separately, it is hoped that each little volume may be found attractive and companionable; while taken together, they will, if they fulfil the design of Editor and Publisher, afford a pleasant bird's-eye view ranging over nearly five-hundred years of English Song.

With regard to this First Series, it has seemed above all things important that the contents of the book should be choice and various; that no short poem (such as Milton's *Lycidas* or Gray's *Elegy*) which comes down to us stamped with the approval of generations, should be omitted; that fragments, political verses, and everything of a polemic or dramatic character should be deemed foreign to the general plan of the work; and that no poem, however beautiful, which could be supposed to have an objectionable tendency, should find a place in its pages. It is hoped that in so far as care and patience may be trusted to ensure the fulfilment of a long-cherished plan, these conditions have been scrupulously observed.

Concerning the order in which the poems are presented, it must be remembered that a question of arrangement is in fact a question of taste, and that a question of taste will always be open to dispute. Campbell's seven learned volumes of *"Specimens of English Poetry"* follow a chronological order. The well-known *"Elegant Extracts"* are classified under headings "Didactic," "Pastoral," "Amatory," and the like. *"The Golden Treasury,"* unapproachable for exquisite taste and scholarship, is divided into four parts designated as the Books of Shakespeare, Milton, Gray and Wordsworth. The Editor of this present collection has, however, preferred to consider English Poetry under only two aspects, and broadly to separate it into only two epochs—namely the Past and the Present. The Past is held to begin at that critical period when our language, having just passed as it were from the fluid to the crystalline stage, found an exponent in the author of *The Canterbury Tales;* while the Present is dated from the advent of Robert Burns.

Except, then, as the poems in this Series belong to the elder school of English verse, every chronological consideration has been put aside, and the position of each piece determined solely by its relation to that which goes before and after it. Hence Waller and Ben Jonson, William Blake and Beaumont will be found side by side, according as each may illustrate or contrast with the other; while readers who care to observe the attitude of contemporary thought on certain universal subjects, such as Love, or Death, or the Influences of Nature, will elsewhere find grouped together poems which treat of a common theme. These groups, again, are for the most part linked with other groups in such wise as to carry on slight chains of connection between subjects far apart. To the few who may be interested in tracing them, these lines of association will perhaps convey an added sense of harmony; while for those who prefer dipping into the book wherever it may chance to open, each poem will have its individual and unassisted charm. Here and there, to suggest the intended sequence, the Editor, following the precedent of Mr. W. G. Palgrave,* has ventured, though with all diffidence, to give or alter a title. It may be as well to observe, however, that readers who desire to take the poets in strict order of

---

* Some few of the titles here given are adopted from *The Golden Treasury*, and some of Mr. W. G. Palgrave's Notes, with due acknowledgment, have been quoted.

succession, may do so by referring to the Table of Authors which has been chronologically arranged for that purpose.

The notes at the end of the volume are given, not in the vain hope of offering anything new in the way of criticism, but in order to assist foreign readers, and to supply the place of those classical and other dictionaries which travellers are obliged to leave at home.

Lastly, as regards the title of the book, some apology should perhaps be offered for its exceeding homeliness. But the taste for high-sounding titles has passed away; and the changes have been rung so long and so often upon "Gems," "Beauties," "Wreaths," "Caskets," and the like, that it is believed the old, plain, familiar nursery-name by which we have all designated the "poetry-books" of our childhood will find more favour, and call up pleasanter associations, than a more fanciful or elaborate title.

AMELIA B. EDWARDS.

Westbury on Trym,
Gloucestershire, Novr 1877.

CONTENTS.

CONTENTS.

XIII

ELDER ENGLISH POETS.

LOVE-LONGING.

[AUTHOR UNKNOWN:—CIRCA A.D. 1300.]

FOR hir loue I carke and care,
For hir loue I droope and dare
For hir alle my blisse is bare,
    And I wex wan.

For hir loue in slepe I slake,
For hir loue alle nighte I wake,
For hir loue I mournynge make
    More than any man.

RONDEAU.

I.

1.

YOURE two eyn will sle me sodenly,
I may the beauté of them not sustene,
So wendeth it thorowout my herté kene

2.

And but your words will helen hastely
My hertis wound, while that it is grene,
Youre two eyn will sle me sodenly.

3.

Upon my trouth I sey yow feithfully,
That ye ben of my liffe and deth the quene;
For with my deth the trouth shal be sene.
    Youre two eyn, &c.

1 *

II.

1.

So hath youre beauté fro your herté chased
Pitee, that me n'availeth not to pleyn:
For daunger halt youre mercy in his cheyne.

2.

Giltless my deth thus have ye purchased;
I sey yow soth, me nedeth not to fayn:
So hath youre beauté fro your herté chased.

3.

Alas, that nature hath in yow compassed
So grete beauté that no man may atteyn
To mercy, though he sterve for the peyn.
   So hath youre beauté &c.

III.

1.

Syn I fro love escapèd am so fat,
I nere thinke to ben in his prison lene;
Syn I am fre, I count hym not a bene.

2.

He may answere, and sey this and that,
I do no fors, I speke ryght as I mene;
Syn I fro love escaped am so fat.

3.

Love hath my name i-strike out of his sclat,
And he is strike out of my bokés clene:
For ever mo ther is non other mene,
   Syn I fro love escapèd &c.

Geoffrey Chaucer.

TO LIFE'S PILGRIM.

FLY from the press, and dwell with soothfastness;
  Suffice unto thy good, though it be small,
For hoard hath hate, and climbing tickleness;
  Preise hath envie, and weal is blent o'er all.
  Savor no more than thee behoven shall,
Rede well thy self that other folk can'st rede,
And Truth thee shalt deliver—'tis no drede.

That thee is sent receive in buxomness:
  The wrestling of this world, asketh a fall.
Here is no home, here is but wilderness.
  Forth, pilgrim, forth—on, best out of thy stall;
  Look up on high, and thank the God of all!
Weivith thy lust, and let thy ghost thee lead,
And Truth thee shalt deliver—'tis no drede.

G. Chaucer.

TO MAISTRES MARGARETE.

1.

MIRRY Margaret
As midsomer flowre,
Gentil as faucoun
Or hauke of the towre;
  With solace and gladnes
  Moch mirth and no madnes
  All good and no badnes

So joyously,
So maydenly,
So womanly
Her demenynge
In every thynge,
Far, far passynge
That I can endite
Or suffice to write
Of mirry Margarete
As midsomer flowre
Gentil as faucoun
Or hauke of the towre!

2.

As pacient and as styll
And as ful of good wil
As fayre Isiphill,
Coliander,
Swete Pomaunder,
Good Cassander,
Stedfast of thought,
Wel made, wel wrought,
Far may be soughte
Erst ye can fynde
So curteise, so kynde
As mirry Margarete
This midsomer flowre,
Gentil as faucoun
Or hauke of the towre!

John Skelton.

MY SWETE SWETYNG.

(TEMPO HENRY VIII.)

AH! my swete swetyng,
My lytyl pretie swetyng!
My swetyng wyl I loue whereuer I goe:
She is soe proper and pure,
Stedfaste, stabyll, and demure,—
There is nonne suche, ye may be sure,
As my swete swetyng.

In all thys worlde, as thynketh mee,
Is nonne soe plesaunte to my 'ee,
That I am gladde soe ofte to see,
As my swete swetynge.

When I beholde my swetyng swete,
Her face, her haundes, her minion fete,
They seeme to mee ther is nonne soe mete
As my swete swetynge.

Above alle others prayse must I,
And loue my pretie pigsnye;
For nonne I finde so womanlie
As my swete swetynge.

She is soe proper and pure,
Stedfaste, stabyll, and demure,—
There is nonne suche, ye may be sure,
As my swete swetynge.

Anonymous.

A CAROL OF SPRING,

WHEREIN ECHE THING RENEWES SAUE ONELY THE LOVER.

THE soote season, that bud and blome forth brings,
With grene hath clad the hill, and eke the vale:
The nightingale with fethers newe she sings:
The turtle to her mate hath tolde her tale:
Somer is come, for euery spray now springs:
The hart hath hong his old hed on the pale;
The bucke in brake his winter coate he flings:
The fishes flete with new repaired scale:
The adder all her slough away she flings;
The swift swalow pursueth the flies smale;
The busy bee her honey now she mings;
Winter is worne, that was the floures bale;
And thus I see among these pleasaunt things
Eche care decayes; and yet my sorow springs.

Henry Howard (Earl of Surrey).

MADRIGAL.

WORSHIP, O ye that lovers be, this May!
  For of your bliss the Calends are begun;
And sing with us, 'Away! winter, away!
  Come, summer, come, the sweet season and sun;'
  Awake for shame that have your heavens won;
    And amorously lift up your headës all,
    Thank Love that list you to his mercy call!

King James I. (of Scotland).

SPRING.

SPRING, the sweet Spring, is the year's pleasant king;
Then blooms each thing, then maids dance in a ring,
Cold doth not sting, the pretty birds do sing,
    Cuckoo, jug-jug, pu-we, to-witta-woo!

The palm and may make country houses gay,
Lambs frisk and play, the shepherds pipe all day,
And we hear aye birds tune this merry lay,
    Cuckoo, jug-jug, pu-we, to-witta-woo.

The fields breathe sweet, the daisies kiss our feet,
Young lovers meet, old wives a sunning sit,
In every street these tunes our ears do greet,
    Cuckoo, jug-jug, pu-we, to-witta-woo!
        Spring! the sweet Spring!
                Thomas Nash.

THE PASSIONATE SHEPHERD TO HIS LOVE.

COME live with me and be my Love,
And we will all the pleasures prove
That hills and valleys, dale and field,
And all the craggy mountains yield.

There will we sit upon the rocks
And see the shepherds feed their flocks,
By shallow rivers, to whose falls
Melodious birds sing madrigals.

There will I make thee beds of roses
And a thousand fragrant posies,
A cap of flowers, and a kirtle
Embroider'd all with leaves of myrtle.

A gown made of the finest wool,
Which from our pretty lambs we pull,
Fair linéd slippers for the cold,
With buckles of the purest gold.

A belt of straw and ivy buds
With coral clasps and amber studs:
And if these pleasures may thee move,
Come live with me and be my Love.

Thy silver dishes for thy meat
As precious as the gods do eat,
Shall on an ivory table be
Prepared each day for thee and me.

The shepherd swains shall dance and sing
For thy delight each May-morning:
If these delights thy mind may move,
Then live with me and be my Love.

Christopher Marlowe.

THE SHEPHERDESS'S REPLY.

IF all the world and love were young,
And truth in every shepherd's tongue,
These pretty pleasures might me move
To live with thee and be thy love;

But time drives flocks from field to fold,
When rivers rage and rocks grow cold,
Then Philomel becometh dumb,
And age complains of cares to come.

The flowers do fade, and wanton fields
To wayward winter reckoning yields;
A honey tongue, a heart of gall,
Is fancy's spring, but sorrow's fall.

Thy gowns, thy shoes, thy beds of roses,
Thy cap, thy kirtle, and thy posies,
Soon break, soon wither, soon forgotten;
In folly ripe, in reason rotten.

Thy belt of straw and ivy-buds,
Thy coral clasps and amber studs,
All these in me no means can move,
To come to thee and be thy love.

What should we talk of dainties, then,
Of better meat than's fit for men?   .
These are but vain: that's only good
Which God hath bless'd and sent for food.

But could youth last, and love still breed,
Had joys no date, nor age no need;
Then those delights my mind might move,
To live with thee and be thy love.

Sir Walter Raleigh.

SAMELA.

LIKE to Diana in her summer weed,
Girt with a crimson robe of brightest dye,
      Goes fair Samela!
Whiter than be the flocks that straggling feed,
When washed by Arethusa faint they lie,
      Is fair Samela!
As fair Aurora in her morning gray,
Decked with the ruddy glister of her love,
      Is fair Samela!
Like lovely Thetis on a calméd day,
Whenas her brightness Neptune's fancies move,
      Shines fair Samela!
Her tresses gold, her eyes like glassy streams;
Her teeth are pearl, the breasts are ivory
      Of fair Samela!
Her cheeks, like rose and lily, yield forth gleams;
Her brows' bright arches framed of ebony:
      Thus fair Samela
Passeth fair Venus in her bravest hue,
And Juno in the show of majesty,
      For she's Samela!
Pallas in wit,—all three, if you will view,
For beauty, wit, and matchless dignity,
      Yield to Samela.

Robert Greene.

TO HIS LADY.

Ask me no more where Jove bestows,
When June is past, the fading rose;
For in your beauties' orient deep,
These flow'rs, as in their causes, sleep.

Ask me no more, whither do stray
The golden atoms of the day;
For, in pure love, heaven did prepare
Those powders to enrich your hair.

Ask me no more, whither doth haste
The nightingale, when May is past;
For in your sweet dividing throat
She winters, and keeps warm her note.

Ask me no more, where those stars light,
That downwards fall in dead of night;
For, in your eyes they sit, and there
Fixèd become, as in their sphere.

Ask me no more, if east or west,
The phœnix builds her spicy nest;
For unto you at last she flies,
And in your fragrant bosom dies.

Thomas Carew.

CUPID AND CAMPASPE.

CUPID and my Campaspe play'd
At cards for kisses; Cupid paid:
He stakes his quiver, bow, and arrows,
His mother's doves, and team of sparrows;
Loses them too; then down he throws
The coral of his lip, the rose
Growing on's cheek (but none knows how);
With these, the crystal of his brow,
And then the dimple on his chin;
All these did my Campaspe win:
At last he set her both his eyes—
She won, and Cupid blind did rise.
    O Love! has she done this to thee?
    What shall, alas! become of me?

John Lylye.

TO CELIA.

1.

DRINK to me only with thine eyes,
  And I will pledge with mine;
Or leave a kiss within the cup,
  And I'll not look for wine.
The thirst that from the soul doth rise,
  Doth ask a drink divine:
But might I of Jove's nectar sup,
  I would not change for thine.

2.

I sent thee late a rosy wreath,
  Not so much honouring thee,
As giving it a hope, that there
  It could not withered be;
But thou thereon didst only breathe,
  And sent'st it back to me,
Since when it grows, and smells, I swear,
  Not of itself but thee.

Ben Jonson.

KISSING THE AIR.

I DARE not ask a kiss,
    I dare not beg a smile;
Lest, having that or this,
    I might grow proud the while.

No, no! the utmost share
    Of my desire shall be,
Only to kiss the air
    That late kissed thee.

Robert Herrick.

A DITTY.

MY true-love hath my heart, and I have his,
By just exchange one to the other given:
I hold his dear, and mine he cannot miss,
There never was a better bargain driven:
    My true-love hath my heart, and I have his.

His heart in me keeps him and me in one,
My heart in him his thoughts and senses guides:
He loves my heart, for once it was his own,
I cherish his because in me it bides:
    My true-love hath my heart, and I have his.

Sir Philip Sidney.

THE LOVER GROWETH OLD.

THAT time of year thou may'st in me behold
When yellow leaves, or none, or few do hang
Upon those boughs which shake against the cold,
Bare ruin'd choirs, where late the sweet birds sang.

In me thou seest the twilight of such day
As after sunset fadeth in the west,
Which by and by black night doth take away,
Death's second self, that seals up all in rest.

In me thou seest the glowing of such fire,
That on the ashes of his youth doth lie
As the deathbed whereon it must expire,
Consumed with that which it was nourish'd by:

—-This thou perceiv'st, which makes thy love more strong,
To love that well which thou must leave ere long.

LOVE SEETH NO CHANGE.

To me, fair Friend, you never can be old,
For as you were when first your eye I eyed
Such seems your beauty still.   Three winters cold
Have from the forests shook three summers' pride;

Three beauteous springs to yellow autumn turn'd
In process of the season have I seen,
Three April perfumes in three hot Junes burn'd,
Since first I saw you fresh which yet are green.

Ah! yet doth beauty, like a dial hand,
Steal from his figure, and no pace perceived;
So your sweet hue, which methinks still doth stand,
Hath motion, and mine eye may be deceived:

For fear of which, hear this, thou age unbred,—
Ere you were born, was beauty's summer dead.

W. Shakespeare.

THE LOVER PROMISETH IMMORTALITY.

SHALL I compare thee to a summer's day?
Thou art more lovely and more temperate:
Rough winds do shake the darling buds of May,
And summer's lease hath all too short a date:

Sometime too hot the eye of heaven shines,
And often is his gold complexion dimm'd:
And every fair from fair sometime declines,
By chance, or nature's changing course, untrimm'd.

But thy eternal summer shall not fade
Nor lose possession of that fair thou owest;
Nor shall death brag thou wanderest in his shade,
When in eternal lines to time thou growest.

So long as men can breathe, or eyes can see,
So long lives this, and this gives life to thee.

W. Shakespeare.

LOVE IN ABSENCE.

LIKE as the culver on the barèd bough
Sits mourning for the absence of her mate,
And in her songs sends many a wishful vow
For his return, that seems to linger late;
So I alone, now left disconsolate,
Mourn to myself the absence of my love,
And wandering here and there all desolate,
Seek with my plaints to match that mournful dove.
Ne joy of aught that under heaven doth hove
Can comfort me, but her own joyous sight
Whose sweet aspect both god and man can move
In her unspotted pleasance to delight:
And in the heavens write your glorious name,
Where, when as Death shall all the world subdue,
Our love shall live, and later life renew.

Edmund Spenser.

THE NIGHTINGALE.

As it fell upon a day
In the merry month of May,
Sitting in a pleasant shade
Which a grove of myrtles made,
Beasts did leap and birds did sing,
Trees did grow and plants did spring,
Every thing did banish moan
Save the nightingale alone.
She, poor bird, as all forlorn,
Lean'd her breast against a thorn,
And there sung the dolefullest ditty
That to hear it was great pity.
Fie, fie, fie, now would she cry;
Tereu, tereu, by and by:
That to hear her so complain
Scarce I could from tears refrain;
For her griefs so lively shown
Made me think upon mine own.
—Ah, thought I, thou mournst in vain,
None takes pity on thy pain:
Senseless trees, they cannot hear thee,
Ruthless beasts, they will not cheer thee;
King Pandion, he is dead,
All thy friends are lapp'd in lead:
All thy fellow birds do sing
Careless of thy sorrowing:
Even so, poor bird, like thee
None alive will pity me.

Richard Barnefield.

LOVE'S PERJURIES.

ON a day, alack the day!
Love, whose month is ever May,
Spied a blossom passing fair
Playing in the wanton air:
Through the velvet leaves the wind
All unseen 'gan passage find;
That the lover, sick to death,
Wish'd himself the heaven's breath.
Air, quoth he, thy cheeks may blow;
Air, would I might triumph so!
But, alack, my hand is sworn
Ne'er to pluck thee from thy thorn:
Vow, alack, for youth unmeet;
Youth so apt to pluck a sweet.
Do not call it sin in me
That I am forsworn for thee:
Thou for whom e'en Jove would swear
Juno but an Ethiope were,
And deny himself for Jove,
Turning mortal for thy love.

W. Shakespeare.

THE LOVER'S APPEAL.

AND wilt thou leave me thus?
Say nay! say nay! for shame,
To save thee from the blame
Of all my grief and grame.
And wilt thou leave me thus?
Say nay! say nay!

And wilt thou leave me thus,
That hath loved thee so long
In wealth and woe among:
And is thy heart so strong
As for to leave me thus?
Say nay! say nay!

And wilt thou leave me thus,
That hath given thee my heart
Never for to depart
Neither for pain nor smart:
And wilt thou leave me thus?
Say nay! say nay!

And wilt thou leave me thus,
And have no more pity
Of him that loveth thee?
Alas! thy cruelty!
And wilt thou leave me thus?
Say nay! say nay!

Sir Thomas Wyatt.

LOVE'S LAST MOMENTS.

Since there's no help, come let us kiss and part,—
Nay I have done, you get no more of me;
And I am glad, yea glad with all my heart,
That thus so cleanly I myself can free;

Shake hands for ever, cancel all our vows,
And when we meet at any time again,
Be it not seen in either of our brows
That we one jot of former love retain.

Now at the last gasp of love's latest breath,
When his pulse failing, passion speechless lies,
When faith is kneeling by his bed of death,
And innocence is closing up his eyes,

—Now if thou would'st, when all have given him over,
From death to life thou might'st him yet recover!

Michael Drayton.

TO THE MOON.

WITH how sad steps, O Moon, thou climb'st the skies!
How silently, and with how wan a face!
What!—may it be, that ev'n in heavenly place
That busy archer his sharp arrows tries?
Sure, if that long-with-love-acquainted eyes
Can judge of love, thou feel'st a lover's case;
I read it in thy looks; thy languished grace,
To me that feel the like, thy state descries.
Then, ev'n of fellowship, O Moon, tell me,
Is constant love deemed there but want of wit?
Are beauties there as proud as here they be?
Do they above love to be loved, and yet
Those lovers scorn, whom that love doth possess?
Do they call virtue there—ungratefulness?

Sir P. Sidney.

TO THE NIGHTINGALE.

O NIGHTINGALE, that on yon bloomy spray
    Warblest at eve, when all the woods are still,
    Thou with fresh hope the lover's heart does fill,
    While the jolly Hours lead on propitious May.
Thy liquid notes that close the eye of day,
    First heard before the shallow cuckoo's bill,
    Portend success in love; O, if Jove's will
    Have link'd that amorous power to thy soft lay,
Now timely sing, e'er the rude bird of hate
    Foretell my hopeless doom in some grove nigh;
    As thou from year to year hast sung too late
For my relief, yet hadst no reason why:
    Whether the muse, or love call thee his mate,
    Both them I serve, and of their train am I.

John Milton.

TO HIS LUTE.

My lute, be as thou wert when thou didst grow
With thy green mother in some shady grove,
When immelodious winds but made thee move,
And birds their ramage did on thee bestow.

Since that dear Voice which did thy sounds approve,
Which wont in such harmonious strains to flow,
Is reft from Earth to tune those spheres above,
What art thou but a harbinger of woe?

Thy pleasing notes be pleasing notes no more,
But orphans' wailings to the fainting ear;
Each stroke a sigh, each sound draws forth a tear;
For which be silent as in woods before:

Or if that any hand to touch thee deign,
Like widow'd turtle still her loss complain.

William Drummond.

THE LOVER TO HIS LYRE.

AWAKE, awake, my Lyre!
And tell thy silent master's humble tale
  In sounds that may prevail,—
  Sounds that gentle thoughts inspire:
    Though so exalted she
    And I so lowly be,
Tell her such different notes make all thy harmony.

  Hark! how the strings awake;
And though the moving hand approach not near,
  Themselves with awful fear
  A kind of numerous trembling make.
    Now all thy forces try;
    Now all thy charms apply:
Revenge upon her ear the conquests of her eye!

  Weak Lyre! thy virtue sure
Is useless here, since thou art only found
  To cure, but not to wound—
  And she to wound, but not to cure.
    Too weak too wilt thou prove,
    My passion to remove:
Physic to other ills, thou'rt nourishment to love.

  Sleep, sleep again, my Lyre!
For thou canst never tell my humble tale
  In sounds that will prevail,
  Nor gentle thoughts in her inspire.
    All thy vain mirth lay by,
    Bid thy strings silent lie:
Sleep, sleep again, my Lyre, and let thy master die!

Abraham Cowley.

LAMENT FOR ASTROPHEL.*

"Woods, hills, and rivers, now are desolate,
 Sith he is gone, the which them all did grace;
 And all the fields do wail their widow state,
 Sith death their fairest flower did late deface:
 The fairest flower in field that ever grew
 Was Astrophel; that was we all may rue.

"What cruel hand of cursed foe unknown
 Hath cropt the stalk which bore so fair a flower?
 Untimely cropt, before it well were grown,
 And clean defaced in untimely hour;
 Great loss to all that ever him did see,
 Great loss to all, but greatest loss to me.

"Break now your girlonds, O ye shepherds' lasses!
 Sith the fair flower which them adorn'd is gone;
 The flower which them adorn'd is gone to ashes,
 Never again let lass put girlond on:
 Instead of girlond wear sad cypress now,
 And bitter elder broken from the bough.

"Ne ever sing the love-lays which he made;
 Who ever made such lays of love as he?
 Ne ever read the riddles which he said
 Unto yourselves to make you merry glee:
 Your merry glee is now laid all abed,
 Your merry maker now, alas! is dead.

* Sir Philip Sidney.

" Death, the devourer of all world's delight,
  Hath robbed you, and reft fro me my joy;
  Both you and me, and all the world, he quite
  Hath robb'd of joyance, and left sad annoy.
  Joy of the world, and shepherds' pride, was he;
  Shepherds, hope never like again to see.

"O Death! that hast us of such riches reft,
  Tell us, at least, what hast thou with it done?
  What is become of him whose flower here left
  Is but the shadow of his likeness gone?
  Scarce like the shadow of that which he was,
  Nought like, but that he like a shade did pass.

"But that immortal spirit, which was deck'd
  With all the dowries of celestial grace,
  By sovereign choice from th' heavenly quires select,
  And lineally deriv'd from angels' race,
  O what is now of it become? aread:
  Aye me! can so divine a thing be dead:

"Ah! no: it is not dead, ne can it die,
  But lives for aye in blissful paradise,
  Where like a new-born babe it soft doth lie
  In bed of lilies, wrapt in tender wise,
  And compass'd all·about with roses sweet,
  And dainty violets from head to feet.

"There thousand birds, all of celestial brood,
  To him do sweetly carol day and night,
  And with strange notes, of him well understood,
  Lull him asleep in angel-like delight;
  Whilst in sweet dream to him presented be
  Immortal beauties, which no eye may see.

"But he them sees, and takes exceeding pleasure
　　Of their divine aspects, appearing plain,
　　And kindling love in him above all measure;
　　Sweet love, still joyous, never feeling pain:
　　For what so goodly form he there doth see
　　He may enjoy, from jealous rancour free.

" There liveth he in everlasting bliss,
　　Sweet Spirit! never fearing more to die,
　　Ne dreading harm from any foes of his,
　　Ne fearing savage beasts' more cruelty,
　　Whilst we here wretches wail his private lack,
　　And with vain vows do often call him back.

"But live thou there still, happy, happy Spirit!
　　And give us leave thee here thus to lament;
　　Not thee that dost thy heaven's joy inherit,
　　But our own selves, that here in dole are drent.
　　Thus do we weep and wail, and wear our eyes,
　　Mourning in others our own miseries."

E. Spenser.

THE SHEPHERD'S ELEGY.

GLIDE soft ye silver floods,
  And every spring:
Within the shady woods
  Let no bird sing!
Nor from the grove a turtle dove
Be seen to couple with her love;
But silence on each dale and mountain dwell,
Whilst Willy bids his friend and joy farewell.

But (of great Thetis' train)
  Ye mermaids fair,
That on the shores do plain
  Your sea-green hair,
As ye in trammels knit your locks
Weep ye; and so enforce the rocks
In heavy murmurs through the broad shores tell
How Willy bade his friend and joy farewell.

Cease, cease, ye murmuring winds
  To move a wave;
But if with troubled minds
  You seek his grave,
Know 'tis as various as yourselves,
Now in the deep, then on the shelves,
His coffin toss'd by fish and surges fell,
Whilst Willy weeps and bids all joy farewell.

Had he, Arion like,
    Been judg'd to drown,
He on his lute could strike
    So rare a swon;
A thousand dolphins would have come,
    And jointly strove to bring him home.
But he on shipboard dy'd, by sickness fell,
Since when his Willy bade all joy farewell.

Great Neptune hear a swain!
    His coffin take,
And with a golden chain
    (For pity) make
It fast unto a rock near land!
    Where ev'ry calmy morn I'll stand,
And ere one sheep out of my flock I tell,
Sad Willy's pipe shall bid his friend farewell.

William Browne.

LYCIDAS.

ELEGY ON A FRIEND DROWNED IN THE IRISH CHANNEL.

YET once more, O ye laurels, and once more,
Ye myrtles brown, with ivy never sere,
I come, to pluck your berries harsh and crude;
And, with forced fingers rude,
Shatter your leaves before the mellowing year.
Bitter constraint, and sad occasion dear
Compels me to disturb your season due:
For Lycidas is dead, dead ere his prime,
Young Lycidas, and hath not left his peer:
Who would not sing for Lycidas? he knew
Himself to sing, and build the lofty rhyme.
He must not float upon his watery bier
Unwept, and welter to the parching wind,
Without the meed of some melodious tear.

    Begin then, Sisters of the sacred well
That from beneath the seat of Jove doth spring,
Begin, and somewhat loudly sweep the string;
Hence with denial vain and coy excuse:
So may some gentle Muse
With lucky words favour my destined urn;
And as he passes, turn
And bid fair peace be to my sable shroud.

    For we were nursed upon the self-same hill,
Fed the same flock by fountain, shade, and rill.

Together both, ere the high lawns appear'd
Under the opening eye-lids of the morn,
We drove a-field, and both together heard
What time the gray fly winds her sultry horn,
Battening our flocks with the fresh dews of night;
Oft till the star, that rose at evening bright,
Toward heaven's descent had sloped his westering wheel.
Meanwhile the rural ditties were not mute,
Temper'd to the oaten flute;
Rough Satyrs danced, and Fauns with cloven heel
From the glad sound would not be absent long;
And old Damoetas loved to hear our song.

But, O the heavy change, now thou art gone,
Now thou art gone, and never must return!
Thee, Shepherd, thee the woods, and desert caves
With wild thyme and the gadding vine o'ergrown,
And all their echoes, mourn:
The willows and the hazel copses green
Shall now no more be seen
Fanning their joyous leaves to thy soft lays:—
As killing as the canker to the rose,
Or taint-worm to the weanling herds that graze,
Or frost to flowers, that their gay wardrobe wear,
When first the white-thorn blows;
Such, Lycidas, thy loss to shepherds' ear.

Where were ye, Nymphs, when the remorseless deep
Closed o'er the head of your loved Lycidas?
For neither were ye playing on the steep
Where your old bards, the famous Druids, lie,
Nor on the shaggy top of Mona high,
Nor yet where Deva spreads her wizard stream:
Ay me! I fondly dream—
Had ye been there—for what could that have done?
What could the Muse herself that Orpheus bore,
The Muse herself, for her enchanting son,

Whom universal nature did lament,
When by the rout that made the hideous roar
His gory visage down the stream was sent,
Down the swift Hebrus to the Lesbian shore?

   Alas! what boots it with incessant care
To tend the homely, slighted, shepherd's trade
And strictly meditate the thankless Muse?
Were it not better done, as others use,
To sport with Amaryllis in the shade,
Or with the tangles of Neaera's hair?
Fame is the spur that the clear spirit doth raise
(That last infirmity of noble mind)
To scorn delights, and live laborious days;
But the fair guerdon when we hope to find,
And think to burst out into sudden blaze,
Comes the blind Fury with the abhorréd shears
And slits the thin-spun life. "But not the praise"
Phoebus replied, and touch'd my trembling ears;
"Fame is no plant that grows on mortal soil,
Nor in the glistering foil
Set off to the world, nor in broad rumour lies:
But lives and spreads aloft by those pure eyes
And perfect witness of all-judging Jove;
As he pronounces lastly on each deed,
Of so much fame in heaven expect thy meed."

   O fountain Arethuse, and thou honour'd flood
Smooth-sliding Mincius, crown'd with vocal reeds!
That strain I heard was of a higher mood:
But now my oat proceeds,
And listens to the herald of the sea
That came in Neptune's plea;
He ask'd the waves, and ask'd the felon winds,
What hard mishap hath doom'd this gentle swain?
And question'd every gust of rugged wings

That blows from off each beakéd promontory:
They knew not of his story;
And sage Hippotadés their answer brings,
That not a blast was from his dungeon stray'd;
The air was calm, and on the level brine
Sleek Panopé with all her sisters play'd.
It was that fatal and perfidious bark
Built in the eclipse, and rigg'd with curses dark,
That sunk so low that sacred head of thine.

Next Camus, reverend sire, went footing slow,
His mantle hairy, and his bonnet sedge
Inwrought with figures dim, ánd on the edge
Like to that sanguine flower inscribed with woe:
"Ah! who hath reft", quoth he, "my dearest pledge!"
Last came, and last did go
The pilot of the Galilean lake;
Two massy keys he bore of metals twain
(The golden opes, the iron shuts amain);
He shook his mitred locks, and stern bespake:
'How well could I have spared for thee, young swain,
Enow of such, as for their bellies' sake
Creep and intrude and climb into the fold!
Of other care they little reckoning make
Than how to scramble at the shearers' feast,
And shove away the worthy bidden guest;
Blind mouths! that scarce themselves know how to hold
A sheep-hook, or have learn'd aught else the least
That to the faithful herdman's art belongs!
What recks it them? What need they? They are sped;
And when they list, their lean and flashy songs
Grate on their scrannel pipes of wretched straw;
The hungry sheep look up, and are not fed,
But swoln with wind and the rank mist they draw
Rot inwardly, and foul contagion spread:
Besides what the grim wolf with privy paw
Daily devours apace, and nothing said:

—But that two-handed engine at the door
Stands ready to smite once, and smite no more."

Return, Alphéus, the dread voice is past
That shrunk thy streams; return, Sicilian Muse,
And call the vales, and bid them hither cast
Their bells and flowerets of a thousand hues.
Ye valleys low, where the mild whispers use
Of shades, and wanton winds, and gushing brooks
On whose fresh lap the swart star sparely looks;
Throw hither all your quaint enamell'd eyes
That on the green turf suck the honey'd showers
And purple all the ground with vernal flowers.
Bring the rathe primrose that forsaken dies,
The tufted crow-toe, and pale jessamine,
The white pink, and the pansy freak'd with jet,
The glowing violet,
The musk-rose, and the well-attired woodbine,
With cowslips wan that hang the pensive head,
And every flower that sad embroidery wears:
Bid amarantus all his beauty shed,
And daffodillies fill their cups with tears
To strew the laureat hearse where Lycid lies.
For, so to interpose a little ease,
Let our frail thoughts dally with false surmise;
Ay me! whilst thee the shores and sounding seas
Wash far away,—where'er thy bones are hurl'd,
Whether beyond the stormy Hebrides
Where thou perhaps, under the whelming tide,
Visitest the bottom of the monstrous world;
Or whether thou, to our moist vows denied,
Sleep'st by the fable of Bellerus old,
Where the great Vision of the guarded mount
Looks towards Namancos and Bayona's hold,
—Look homeward, Angel, now, and melt with ruth:
—And, O ye dolphins, waft the hapless youth!

Weep no more, woeful shepherds, weep no more,
For Lycidas, your sorrow, is not dead,
Sunk though he be beneath the watery floor;
So sinks the day-star in the ocean-bed,
And yet anon repairs his drooping head
And tricks his beams, and with new-spangled ore
Flames in the forehead of the morning sky:
So Lycidas sunk low, but mounted high
Through the dear might of Him that walk'd the waves;
Where, other groves and other streams along,
With nectar pure his oozy locks he laves,
And hears the unexpressive nuptial song
In the blest kingdoms meek of joy and love.
There entertain him all the saints above
In solemn troops, and sweet societies,
That sing, and singing, in their glory move,
And wipe the tears for ever from his eyes.
Now, Lycidas, the shepherds weep no more;
Henceforth thou art the Genius of the shore
In thy large recompense, and shalt be good
To all that wander in that perilous flood.

Thus sang the uncouth swain to the oaks and rills,
While the still morn went out with sandals gray;
He touch'd the tender stops of various quills,
With eager thought warbling his Doric lay:
And now the sun had stretched out all the hills,
And now was dropt into the western bay:
At last he rose, and twitch'd his mantle blue:
To-morrow to fresh woods, and pastures new.

J. Milton.

THE DIRGE OF IMOGEN.

FEAR no more the heat o' the sun
　　Nor the furious winter's rages;
Thou thy worldly task hast done,
　　Home art gone and ta'en thy wages:
Golden lads and girls all must,
As chimney-sweepers, come to dust.

Fear no more the frown o' the great,
　　Thou art past the tyrant's stroke;
Care no more to clothe, and eat;
　　To thee the reed is as the oak:
The sceptre, learning, physic, must
All follow this, and come to dust.

Fear no more the lightning-flash,
　　Nor the all-dreaded thunder-stone;
Fear not slander, censure rash;
　　Thou hast finished joy and moan:
All lovers young, all lovers must
Consign to thee, and come to dust.

No exorciser harm thee!
Nor no witchcraft charm thee!
Ghost unlaid forbear thee!
Nothing ill come near thee!
　　Quiet consummation have;
　　And renownèd be thy grave!

W. Shakespeare.

A SEA DIRGE.

FULL fathom five thy father lies:
    Of his bones are coral made;
Those are pearls that were his eyes:
    Nothing of him that doth fade,
But doth suffer a sea-change
Into something rich and strange;
Sea-nymphs hourly ring his knell:
Hark! now I hear them,—
    Ding, dong, Bell.

W. Shakespeare.

A LAND DIRGE.

CALL for the robin-redbreast and the wren,
Since o'er shady groves they hover
And with leaves and flowers do cover
The friendless bodies of unburied men.
Call unto his funeral dole
The ant, the field-mouse, and the mole
To rear him hillocks that shall keep him warm
And (when gay tombs are robb'd) sustain no harm;
But keep the wolf far thence, that's foe to men,
For with his nails he'll dig them up again.

John Webster.

THE HAPPY LIFE.

MARTIAL, the things that do attain
  The happy life, be these, I find,
The riches left, not got with pain;
  The fruitful ground, the quiet mind;

The equal friend; no grudge, no strife;
  No charge of rule, nor governance;
Without disease, the healthful life;
  The household of continuance;

The mean diet, no delicate fare;
  The wisdom joined with simpleness;
The night dischargéd of all care,
  Where wine the wit may not oppress.

The faithful wife, without debate;
  Such sleeps as may beguile the night;
Contented with thine own estate,
  Ne wish for death, ne fear his might.
                    H. Howard (Earl of Surrey).

THE QUIET LIFE.

HAPPY the man whose wish and care
A few paternal acres bound,
Content to breathe his native air
          In his own ground.

Whose herds with milk, whose fields with bread,
Whose flocks supply him with attire;
Whose trees in summer yield him shade,
          In winter, fire.

Blest, who can unconcern'dly find
Hours, days, and years, slide soft away
In health of body; peace of mind;
          Quiet by day;

Sound sleep by night; study and ease
Together mix'd; sweet recreation,
And innocence, which most does please
          With meditation.

Thus let me live, unseen, unknown;
Thus unlamented let me die;
Steal from the world, and not a stone
          Tell where I lie.

Alexander Pope.

THE LORD OF SELF.

How happy is he born and taught
That serveth not another's will;
Whose armour is his honest thought,
And simple truth his utmost skill!

Whose passions not his masters are,
Whose soul is still prepared for death,
Not tied unto the world with care
Of public fame, or private breath;

Who envies none that chance doth raise,
Or vice.   Who never understood
How deepest wounds are given by praise;
Nor rules of state; but rules of good:

Who hath his life from rumours freed;
Whose conscience is his strong retreat;
Whose state can neither flatterers feed,
Nor ruin make accusers great;

Who God doth late and early pray
More of his grace than gifts to lend;
And entertains the harmless day
With a well-chosen book or friend;

—This Man is freed from servile bands
Of hope to rise, or fear to fall;
Lord of himself, though not of lands,
And having nothing, yet hath All.

Sir Henry Wotton.

THE MODERATE WISHER.

THIS only grant me, that my means may lie
Too low for envy, for contempt too high.
　　　　　Some honour I would have,
Not from great deeds, but good alone;
Th' unknown are better than ill-known.
　　　　　Rumour can ope the grave:
Acquaintance I would have; but when't depends
Not on the number, but the choice of friends.

Books should, not business, entertain the light,
And sleep, as undisturb'd as death, the night.
　　　　　My house a cottage, more
Than palace, and should fitting be
For all my use; no luxury.
　　　　　My garden painted o'er
With Nature's hand, not Art's; and pleasures yield,
Horace might envy in his Sabine field.

Thus would I double my life's fading space,
For he that runs it well, twice runs his race.
　　　　　And in this true delight,
These unbought sports, that happy state,
I would not fear nor wish my fate,
　　　　　But boldly say each night,
To-morrow let my sun his beams display,
Or in clouds hide them; I have liv'd to-day.

A. Cowley.

THE STEDFAST LIFE.

WHO is the honest man?
He that doth still, and strongly, good pursue;
To God, his neighbour, and himself most true.
   Whom neither force nor fawning can
Unpin, or wrench from giving all their due.

   Whose honesty is not
So loose or easy that a ruffling wind
Can blow away, or glitt'ring look it blind.
   Who rides his sure and even trot,
While the world now rides by, now lags behind.

   Who, when great trials come,
Nor seeks, nor shuns them; but doth calmly stay
Till he the thing, and the example weigh.
   All being brought into a sum,
What place, or person calls for, he doth pay.

   Whom none can work, or woo,
To use in any thing a trick or sleight;
For above all things he abhors deceit.
   His words, and works, and fashion, too,
All of one piece; and all are clear and straight.

   Who never melts or thaws
At close temptations. When the day is done,
His goodness sets not, but in dark can run.
   The sun to others writeth laws,
And is their virtue. Virtue is *his* sun.

Who, when he is to treat
With sick folks, women, those whom passions sway,
Allows for that, and keeps his constant way.
Whom others' faults do not defeat;
But though men fail him, yet his part doth play.

Whom nothing can procure,
When the wide world runs bias, from his will
To writhe his limbs; and share, not mend, the ill.
This is the mark-man, safe and sure,
Who still is right, and prays to be so still.

George Herbert.

THE PERFECT LIFE.

IT is not growing like a tree
In bulk, doth make Man better be;
Or standing long an oak, three hundred year,
To fall a log at last, dry, bald, and sere:
A lily of a day
Is fairer far in May,
Although it fall and die that night—
It was the plant and flower of Light.
In small proportions we just beauties see;
And in short measures life may perfect be.

B. Jonson.

THE VIRTUOUS SOUL.

Sweet day, so cool, so calm, so bright,
The bridal of the earth and sky,
Sweet dews shall weep thy fall to night,
    For thou must die.
Sweet rose, whose hue, angry and brave,
Bids the rash gazer wipe his eye,
Thy root is ever in its grave,
    And thou must die.
Sweet spring, full of sweet days and roses,
A box where sweets compacted lie,
My music shows you have your closes,
    And all must die.
Only a sweet and virtuous soul,
Like seasoned timber, never gives;
But when the whole world turns to coal,
    Then chiefly lives.

G. Herbert.

THE SWEETNESS OF CONTENT.

ART thou poor, yet hast thou golden slumbers?
Oh, sweet content!
Art thou rich, yet is thy mind perplexed?
Oh, punishment!
Dost thou laugh to see how fools are vexed
To add to golden numbers, golden numbers?
O, sweet content!

Work apace, apace, apace, apace;
Honest labour bears a lovely face;
Then hey noney, noney, hey noney, noney!

Canst drink the waters of the crispèd spring?
O, sweet content!
Swimmest thou in wealth, yet sink'st in thine own tears?
O, punishment!
Then he that patiently want's burden bears,
No burden bears, but is a king, a king!
O, sweet content!

Work apace, apace, apace, apace;
Honest labour bears a lovely face;
Then hey noney, noney, hey noney, noney!

Thomas Dekker.

SWEET OBSCURITY.

SWEET are the thoughts that savour of content:
The quiet mind is richer than a crown:
Sweet are the nights in careless slumber spent:
The poor estate scorns Fortune's angry frown.
Such sweet content, such minds, such sleep, such bliss,
Beggars enjoy, when princes oft do miss.
The homely house that harbours quiet rest,
The cottage that affords nor pride, nor care,
The mean that 'grees with country music best,
The sweet consort of mirth's and music's fare,
Obscurèd life sets down a type of bliss;
A mind content both crown and kingdom is.

Robert Greene.

LIFE.

THE World's a bubble, and the Life of Man
  Less than a span:
In his conception wretched, from the womb
  So to the tomb;
Curst from his cradle, and brought up to years
  With cares and fears.
Who then to frail mortality shall trust,
But limns on water, or but writes in dust.

Yet whilst with sorrow here we live opprest,
　　　　What life is best?
Courts are but only superficial schools
　　　　To dandle fools:
The rural parts are turn'd into a den
　　　　Of savage men:
And where's a city from foul vice so free,
But may be term'd the worst of all the three?

Domestic cares afflict the husband's bed,
　　　　Or pains his head:
Those that live single, take it for a curse,
　　　　Or do things worse:
Some would have children: those that have them, moan
　　　　Or wish them gone:
What is it, then, to have, or have no wife,
But single thraldom, or a double strife?

Our own affections still at home to please
　　　　Is a disease:
To cross the seas to any foreign soil,
　　　　Peril and toil:
Wars with their noise affright us; when they cease,
　　　　We are worse in peace;—
What then remains, but that we still should cry
For being born, or, being born, to die?

Lord Bacon.

LIFE A BUBBLE.

THIS Life, which seems so fair,
Is like a bubble blown up in the air
By sporting children's breath,
Who chase it every where
And strive who can most motion it bequeath.
And though it sometimes seem of its own might
Like to an eye of gold to be fix'd there,
And firm to hover in that empty height,
That only is because it is so light.
—But in that pomp it doth not long appear;
For when 'tis most admired, in a thought,
Because it erst was nought, it turns to nought.

W. Drummond.

THE LIFE OF MAN.

LIKE to the falling off a star,
Or as the flights of eagles are,
Or like the fresh spring's gaudy hue,
Or silver drops of morning dew,
Or like a wind that chafes the flood,
Or bubbles which on water stood:
Even such is man, whose borrowed light
Is straight called in and paid to night:
The wind blowes out; the bubble dies;
The spring intomb'd in autumn lies;
The dew's dry'd up; the star is shot;
The flight is past; and man forgot!

Francis Beaumont.

MAN'S MORTALITY.

LIKE as the damask rose you see,
Or like the blossom on the tree,
Or like the dainty flower in May,
Or like the morning of the day,
Or like the sun, or like the shade,
Or like the gourd which Jonas had.
E'en such is man; whose thread is spun,
Drawn out, and cut, and so is done.
The rose withers, the blossom blasteth;
The flower fades, the morning hasteth;
The sun sets, the shadow flies;
The gourd consumes,—and man he dies!

Like to the grass that's newly sprung,
Or like a tale that's new begun,
Or like the bird that's here to-day,
Or like the pearlèd dew of May,
Or like an hour, or like a span,
Or like the singing of a swan.
E'en such is man; who lives by breath,
Is here, now there, in life and death.
The grass withers, the tale is ended;
The bird is flown, the dew's ascended;
The hour is short, the span is long;
The swan's near death,—man's life is done!

Simon Wastell.

LIFE'S BREVITY.

MARK that swift arrow! how it cuts the air,
  How it outruns thy following eye!
  Use all persuasions now, and try
If thou canst call it back, or stay it there.
  That way it went; but thou shalt find
  No track is left behind.
Fool! 'tis thy life, and the fond archer thou.
  Of all the time thou'st shot away,
  I'll bid thee fetch but yesterday,
And it shall be too hard a task to do.
  Besides repentance, what canst find
  That it hath left behind?
Our life is carried with too strong a tide;
  A doubtful cloud our substance bears,
  And is the horse of all our years.
Each day doth on a wingèd whirlwind ride.
  We and our glass run out, and must
  Both render up our dust.
But his past life who without grief can see;
  Who never thinks his end too near;
  But says to Fame, "Thou art mine heir;"
That man extends life's natural brevity—
  This is, this is the only way
  To outlive Nestor in a day.

A. Cowley.

SIC VITÆ.

WHAT is the existence of man's life,
But open war or slumber'd strife;
Where sickness to his sense presents
The combat of the elements;
And never feels a perfect peace
Till Death's cold hand signs his release?

It is a storm—where the hot blood
Outvies in rage the boiling flood;
And each loose passion of the mind
Is like a furious gust of wind,
Which beats his bark with many a wave,
Till he casts anchor in the grave.

It is a flower—which buds, and grows,
And withers as the leaves disclose;
Whose spring and fall faint seasons keep,
Like fits of waking before sleep;
Then shrinks into that fatal mould
Where its first being was enroll'd.

It is a dream—whose seeming truth
Is moralised in age and youth;
Where all the comforts he can share
Are wandering as his fancies are;
Till in a mist of dark decay
The dreamer vanish quite away.

SIC VITÆ.

It is a dial—which points out
The sunset, as it moves about;
And shadows out in lines of night
The subtle stages of Time's flight;
Till all-obscuring earth hath laid
His body in perpetual shade.

It is a weary interlude—
Which doth short joys, long woes, include;
The world the stage; the prologue tears;
The acts vain hopes and varied fears;
The scene shuts up with loss of breath,
And leaves no epilogue but death.

Dr. Henry King.

SWEET AND BITTER.

SWEET is the rose, but grows upon a brere;
Sweet is the juniper, but sharp his bough;
Sweet is the eglantine, but pricketh near;
Sweet is the firbloom, but his branches rough;
Sweet is the cyprus, but his rind is tough;
Sweet is the nut, but bitter is his pill;
Sweet is the broom flower, but yet sour enough;
And sweet is moly, but his root is ill;
So, every sweet with sour is tempered still,
That maketh it be coveted the more:
For easy things that may be got at will
Most sorts of men do set but little store.
Why then should I account of little pain,
That endless pleasure shall unto me gain?

E. Spenser.

ILLUSIONS.

A GOOD that never satisfies the mind,
A beauty fading like the April flow'rs,
A sweet with floods of gall, that run combin'd,
A pleasure passing ere in thought made ours,
An honour that more fickle is than wind,
A glory at opinion's frown that low'rs,
A treasury which bankrupt time devours,
A knowledge than grave ignorance more blind,
A vain delight our equals to command,
A style of greatness, in effect a dream,
A swelling thought of holding sea and land,
A servile lot, deck'd with a pompous name,
  Are the strange ends we toil for here below,
  Till wisest death make us our errors know.

W. Drummond.

DEATH'S BOUNTIES.

THE longer life the more offence,
The more offence the greater paine,
The greater paine the lesse defence,
The lesse defence the lesser gaine;
The loss of gaine long yll doth trye,
Wherefore come death and let me dye.
The shorter life, less count I finde,
The less account the sooner made,
The account soon made, the merier mind,
The merier mind doth thought evade;
Short life in truth this thing doth trye,
Wherefore come death and let me dye.
Come gentle death, the ebbe of care,
The ebbe of care, the flood of life,
The flood of life, the joyful fare,
The joyful fare, the end of strife,
The end of strife, that thing wish I,
Wherefore come death and let me die.

Sir T. Wyatt.

THE LAST CONQUEROR.

VICTORIOUS men of earth, no more
  Proclaim how wide your empires are;
Though you bind-in every shore
  And your triumphs reach as far
      As night or day,
  Yet you, proud monarchs, must obey
And mingle with forgotten ashes, when
Death calls ye to the crowd of common men.

Devouring Famine, Plague, and War,
  Each able to undo mankind,
Death's servile emissaries are;
  Nor to these alone confined,
      He hath at will
  More quaint and subtle ways to kill;
A smile or kiss, as he will use the art,
Shall have the cunning skill to break a heart.

James Shirley.

DEATH'S TRIUMPH.

THE glories of our birth and state
  Are shadows, not substantial things;
There is no armour against fate:
  Death lays his icy hand on kings.
      Sceptre and crown
      Must tumble down,
  And in the dust be equal made
  With the poor crooked scythe and spade.

Some men with swords may reap the field,
  And plant with laurels where they kill;
But their strong nerves at last must yield,
  They tame but one another still;
      Early or late,
      They stoop to fate,
  And must give up their murmuring breath,
  When they, pale captives! creep to death.

The garlands wither on your brow;
  Then boast no more your mighty deeds;
Upon death's purple altar, now,
  See where the victor victim bleeds!
      All heads must come
      To the cold tomb,
  Only the actions of the just
  Smell sweet and blossom in the dust.

J. Shirley.

CHANCES AND CHANGES.

THE loppèd tree in time may grow again,
  Most naked plants renew both fruit and flower;
The sorriest wight may find release of pain,
  The driest soil suck in some moist'ning shower:
Time goes by turns, and chances change by course,
From foul to fair, from better times to worse.

The sea of Fortune doth not ever flow;
  She draws her favours to the lowest ebb;
Her tides have equal times to come and go;
  Her loom doth weave the fine and coarsest web:
No joy so great but runneth to an end,
No hap so hard but may in fine amend.

Not always full of leaf, nor ever spring,
  Not endless night, yet not eternal day:
The saddest birds a season find to sing,
  The roughest storms a calm may soon allay.
Thus with succeeding turns God tempereth all,
That man may hope to rise, yet fear to fall.

A chance may win that by mischance was lost;
  That net that holds no great, takes little fish;
In some things all, in all things none are crossed;
  Few all they need, but none have all they wish.
Unmingled joys here to no man befall;
Who least, hath some; who most, hath never all.

Robert Southwell.

THE GOLDEN AGE.

HAPPY that first White Age, when we
Liv'd by the earth's mere charity!
  No soft luxurious diet then
  Had effeminated men—
  No other meat, nor wine, had any
  Than the coarse mast, or simple honey;
  And, by the parents' care laid up,
  Cheap berries did the children sup.
  No pompous wear was in those days,
  Of gummy silks or scarlet baize.
  Their beds were on some flowery brink,
  And clear spring water was their drink.
  The shady pine, in the sun's heat,
  Was their cool and known retreat;
  For then 'twas not cut down, but stood
  The youth and glory of the wood.
  The daring sailor with his slaves
  Then had not cut the swelling waves,
  Nor, for desire of foreign store,
  Seen any but his native shore.
  No stirring drum had scar'd that age,
  Nor the shrill trumpet's active rage;
  No wounds by bitter hatred made
  With warm blood soil'd the shining blade;
  For how could hostile madness arm
  An Age of Love to public harm,
  When common Justice none withstood,
  Nor sought rewards for spilling blood?

Oh that at length our Age would raise
Into the temper of those days!
But—worse than Etna's fires—debate
And avarice inflame our state.
Alas! who was it that first found
Gold (hid of purpose) underground—
That sought out pearls, and div'd to find
Such precious perils for mankind?

Henry Vaughan.

SONG OF THE EMIGRANTS IN BERMUDA.

WHERE the remote Bermudas ride
In the ocean's bosom unespied,
From a small boat that row'd along
The listening winds received this song.
"What should we do but sing His praise
That led us through the watery maze
Where He the huge sea monsters wracks
That lift the deep upon their backs,
Unto an isle so long unknown,
And yet far kinder than our own?
He lands us on a grassy stage,
Safe from the storms, and prelate's rage:
He gave us this eternal spring
Which here enamels everything,
And sends the fowls to us in care
On daily visits through the air.
He hangs in shades the orange bright
Like golden lamps in a green night,
And does in the pomegranates close
Jewels more rich than Ormus shows:

He makes the figs our mouths to meet,
And throws the melons at our feet;
But apples plants of such a price,
No tree could ever bear them twice.
With cedars chosen by his hand
From Lebanon he stores the land;
And makes the hollow seas that roar
Proclaim the ambergris on shore.
He cast (of which we rather boast)
The Gospel's pearl upon our coast;
And in these rocks for us did frame
A temple where to sound His name.
O let our voice His praise exalt
Till it arrive at Heaven's vault,
Which then perhaps rebounding may
Echo beyond the Mexique bay!"
—Thus sung they in the English boat
A holy and a cheerful note:
And all the way, to guide their chime,
With falling oars they kept the time.

Andrew Marvell.

PASTORAL.

My banks they are furnished with bees
  Whose murmur invites one to sleep;
My grottoes are shaded with trees,
  And my hills are white over with sheep.
I seldom have met with a loss,
  Such health do my fountains bestow—
My fountains all bordered with moss,
  Where the harebells and violets grow.

Not a pine in my grove is there seen
  But with tendrils of woodbine is bound;
Not a beech's more beautiful green
  But a sweetbrier entwines it around.
Not my fields in the prime of the year
  More charms than my cattle unfold;
Not a brook that is limpid and clear
  But it glitters with fishes of gold.

One would think she might like to retire
  To the bow'r I have labored to rear;
Not a shrub that I heard her admire
  But I hastened and planted it there.
O how sudden the jessamine strove
  With the lilac, to render it gay!
Already it calls for my love,
  To prune the wild branches away.

From the plains, from the woodlands and groves,
  What strains of wild melody flow!
How the nightingales warble their loves
  From thickets of roses that blow!
And when her bright form shall appear,
  Each bird shall harmoniously join
In a concert, so soft and so clear
  As she may not be fond to resign.

I have found out a gift for my fair—
  I have found where the wood-pigeons breed;
But let me that plunder forbear—
  She will say 'twas a barbarous deed.
For he ne'er could be true, she averr'd,
  Who would rob a poor bird of her young;
And I loved her the more when I heard
  Such tenderness fall from her tongue.

I have heard her with sweetness unfold
  How that Pity was due to a dove;
That it ever attended the bold,
  And she called it the sister of Love.
But her words such a pleasure convey,
  So much I her accents adore,
Let her speak, and whatever she say,
  Methinks I should love her the more.

Can a bosom so gentle remain
  Unmoved when her Corydon sighs?
Will a nymph that is fond of the plain,
  These plains and this valley despise?
Dear regions of silence and shade!
  Soft scenes of contentment and ease!
Where I could have pleasingly strayed,
  If aught in her absence could please.

But where does my Phyllida stray?
　　And where are her grots and her bowers?
Are the groves and the valleys as gay,
　　And the shepherds as gentle as ours?
The groves may perhaps be as fair,
　　And the face of the valleys as fine;
The swains may in manners compare—
　　But their love is not equal to mine.

William Shenstone.

MAY-DAY.

GET up, get up for shame! the blooming morn
Upon her wings presents the god unshorn.
　　See how Aurora throws her fair
　　Fresh-quilted colors through the air!
　　Get up, sweet slug-a-bed! and see
　　The dew bespangling herb and tree.
Each flower has wept and bowed toward the east,
Above an hour since, yet you are not drest—
　　Nay, not so much as out of bed,
　　When all the birds have matins said,
　　And sung their thankful hymns: 'tis sin,
　　Nay, profanation, to keep in,
Whenas a thousand virgins on this day
Spring sooner than the lark to fetch in May.

Rise, and put on your foliage, and be seen
To come forth, like the spring-time, fresh and green,
　　And sweet as Flora.　Take no care
　　For jewels for your gown or hair:
　　Fear not, the leaves will strew
　　Gems in abundance upon you;

Besides, the childhood of the day has kept,
Against you come, some orient pearls unwept.
   Come, and receive them while the light
   Hangs on the dew-locks of the night;
   And Titan on the eastern hill
   Retires himself, or else stands still
Till you come forth.   Wash, dress, be brief in praying:
Few beads are best, when once we go a-Maying.

Come, my Corinna, come! and, coming, mark
How each field turns a street, each street a park
   Made green, and trimmed with trees; see how
   Devotion gives each house a bough,
   Or branch; each porch, each door, ere this
   An ark, a tabernacle is,
Made up of white thorn neatly interwove;
As if here were those cooler shades of love.
   Can such delights be in the street
   And open fields, and we not see't?
   Come! we'll abroad, and let's obey
   The proclamation made for May;
And sin no more, as we have done, by staying,
But, my Corinna, come! let's go a-Maying.

There's not a budding boy or girl, this day,
But is got up, and gone to bring in May.
   A deal of youth, ere this, is come
   Back, and with white thorn laden home.
   Some have despatched their cakes and cream
   Before that we have left to dream;
And some have wept and wooed and plighted troth,
And chose their priest, ere we can cast off sloth.
   Many a green gown has been given;
   Many a kiss, both odd and even;
   Many a glance, too, has been sent
   From out the eye, love's firmament;

Many a jest told of the key's betraying
This night, and locks picked: yet w' are not a-Maying.

Come! let us go while we are in our prime,
And take the harmless folly of the time;
   We shall grow old apace, and die
   Before we know our liberty.
   Our life is short, and our days run
   As fast away as does the sun;
And as a vapor, or a drop of rain
Once lost, can ne'er be found again:
   So when or you or I are made
   A fable, song, or fleeting shade,
   All love, all liking, all delight
   Lies drowned with us in endless night.
Then, while time serves, and we are but decaying,
Come, my Corinna, come! let's go a-Maying.

Robert Herrick.

THE FAITHLESS SHEPHERD.

My sheep I neglected, I broke my sheep-hook,
And all the gay haunts of my youth I forsook;
No more for Amynta fresh garlands I wove:
For ambition, I said, would soon cure me of love.
    Oh, what had my youth with ambition to do?
    Why left I Amynta? Why broke I my vow?
    Oh, give me my sheep, and my sheep-hook restore,
    And I'll wander from love and Amynta no more.

Through regions remote in vain do I rove,
And bid the wide ocean secure me from love!
Oh fool! to imagine that aught could subdue
A love so well founded, a passion so true!
    Oh, what had my youth etc.

Alas! 'tis too late at thy fate to repine;
Poor shepherd, Amynta can never be thine:
Thy tears are all fruitless, thy wishes are vain,
The moments neglected return not again.
    Oh, what had my youth etc.

Sir Gilbert Elliot.

WINTER.

WHEN icicles hang by the wall
  And Dick the shepherd blows his nail,
And Tom bears logs into the hall,
  And milk comes frozen home in pail;
When blood is nipt, and ways be foul,
Then nightly sings the staring owl
              Tuwhoo!
Tuwhit! tuwhoo! A merry note!
While greasy Joan doth keel the pot.

When all around the wind doth blow,
  And coughing drowns the parson's saw,
And birds sit brooding in the snow,
  And Marian's nose looks red and raw;
When roasted crabs hiss in the bowl—
Then nightly sings the staring owl
              Tuwhoo!
Tuwhit! tuwhoo! A merry note!
While greasy Joan doth keel the pot.

W. Shakespeare.

JUNE AND JANUARY.

Now that the winter's gone, the earth has lost
Her snow-white robes: and now no more the frost
Candies the grass, or casts an icy cream
Upon the silver lake or crystal stream:
But the warm sun thaws the benumbèd earth
And makes it tender; gives a sacred birth
To the dead swallow; wakes in hollow tree
The drowsy cuckoo and the humble bee.
Now do a choir of chirping Minstrels bring,
In triumph to the world, the youthful Spring;
The valleys, hills, and woods, in rich array,
Welcome the coming of the longed-for May.
Now all things smile—only my love doth lour:
Nor hath the scalding noon-day sun the pow'r
To melt that marble ice which still doth hold
Her heart congeal'd, and makes her pity cold.
The ox which lately did for shelter fly
Into the stall, doth now securely lie
In open fields; and love no more is made
By the fireside; but in the cooler shade
Amyntas now doth with his Chloris sleep
Under a sycamore, and all things keep
Time with the season—only she doth carry
June in her eyes, in her heart January.

T. Carew.

LOVE'S SPRINGTIME.

IT was a lover and his lass
  With a hey and a ho, and a hey-nonino!
That o'er the green cornfield did pass
In the spring time, the only pretty ring time,
When birds do sing hey ding a ding:
  Sweet lovers love the Spring.

Between the acres of the rye
These pretty country folks would lie:

This carol they began that hour,
How that life was but a flower!

And therefore take the present time
  With a hey and a ho and a hey-nonino!
For love is crownéd with the prime
In spring time, the only pretty ring time,
When birds do sing hey ding a ding:
  Sweet lovers love the Spring.

W. Shakespeare.

A SPRING IDYLL.

THIS day, Dame Nature seem'd in love!
The lusty sap began to move;
Fresh juice did stir th'embracing vines;
And birds had drawn their valentines.
Already were the eaves possess'd
With the swift pilgrim's daubèd nest;
The groves already did rejoice
In Philomel's triumphing voice;
The show'rs were short; the weather mild;
The morning fresh; the evening smil'd.
    Joan takes her neat-rubbed pail, and now
She trips to milk the sand-red cow,
Where, for some sturdy foot-ball swain,
She strokes a syllabub or twain.
The fields and garden were beset
With tulip, crocus, violet;
And now, though late, the modest rose
Did more than half a blush disclose.
    Thus all looks gay and full of cheer,
    To welcome the new-liveried year.

Sir H. Wotton.

MAY MORNING.

Now the bright morning star, day's harbinger,
Comes dancing from the East, and leads with her
The flow'ry May, who from her green lap throws
The yellow cowslip, and the pale primrose.
 Hail bounteous May! that dost inspire
 Mirth, and youth, and warm desire;
 Woods and groves are of thy dressing,
 Hill and dale doth boast thy blessing.
Thus we salute thee with our early song,
And welcome thee and wish thee long.

J. Milton.

L'ALLÉGRO.

HENCE, loathéd Melancholy,
 Of Cerberus and blackest Midnight born
In Stygian cave forlorn
 'Mongst horrid shapes, and shrieks, and sights unholy!
Find out some uncouth cell
 Where brooding Darkness spreads his jealous wings
And the night-raven sings;
 There under ebon shades, and low-brow'd rocks
As ragged as thy locks,
 In dark Cimmerian desert ever dwell.

But come, thou Goddess fair and free,
In heaven yclep'd Euphrosyne,
And by men, heart-easing Mirth,
Whom lovely Venus at a birth
With two sister Graces more
To ivy-crownéd Bacchus bore:
Or whether (as some sager sing)
The frolic wind that breathes the spring
Zephyr, with Aurora playing,
As he met her once a-Maying—
There on beds of violets blue
And fresh-blown roses wash'd in dew
Fill'd her with thee, a daughter fair,
So buxom, blithe, and debonair.
　　Haste thee, Nymph, and bring with thee
Jest, and youthful jollity,
Quips, and cranks, and wanton wiles,
Nods, and becks, and wreathéd smiles
Such as hang on Hebe's cheek,
And love to live in dimple sleek;
Sport that wrinkled Care derides,
And Laughter holding both his sides:—
Come, and trip it as you go
On the light fantastic toe;
And in thy right hand lead with thee
The mountain nymph, sweet Liberty;
And if I give thee honour due,
Mirth, admit me of thy crew,
To live with her, and live with thee
In unreprovéd pleasures free;
To hear the lark begin his flight
And singing startle the dull night
From his watch-tower in the skies,
Till the dappled dawn doth rise;
Then to come, in spite of sorrow,
And at my window bid good-morrow

Through the sweetbriar, or the vine,
Or the twisted eglantine:
While the cock with lively din
Scatters the rear of darkness thin,
And to the stack, or the barn-door,
Stoutly struts his dames before:
Oft listening how the hounds and horn
Cheerly rouse the slumbering morn,
From the side of some hoar hill,
Through the high wood echoing shrill.
Sometime walking, not unseen,
By hedge-row elms, on hillocks green,
Right against the eastern gate
Where the great Sun begins his state
Robed in flames and amber light,
The clouds in thousand liveries dight;
While the ploughman, near at hand,
Whistles o'er the furrow'd land,
And the milkmaid singeth blithe,
And the mower whets his scythe,
And ev'ry shepherd tells his tale
Under the hawthorn in the dale.
  Straight mine eye hath caught new pleasures,
While the landscape round it measures,
Russet lawns, and fallows gray,
Where the nibbling flocks do stray;
Mountains on whose barren breast
The lab'ring clouds do often rest;
Meadows trim with daisies pied;
Shallow brooks, and rivers wide:
Tow'rs and battlements it sees
Bosom'd high in tufted trees,
Where perhaps some beauty lies,
The cynosure of neighb'ring eyes.
Hard by, a cottage-chimney smokes,
From betwixt two aged oaks,

Where Corydon and Thyrsis met,
Are at their sav'ry dinner set
Of herbs, and other country messes,
Which the neat-handed Phyllis dresses:
And then in haste her bow'r she leaves,
With Thestylis to bind the sheaves;
Or, if the earlier season lead,
To the tann'd haycock in the mead.
  Sometimes, with secure delight,
The upland hamlets will invite,
When the merry bells ring round,
And the jocund rebecks sound
To many a youth, and many a maid,
Dancing in the chequer'd shade;
And young and old come forth to play
On a sunshine holiday.
Till the livelong daylight fail;
Then to the spicy nut-brown ale,
With stories told of many a feat,
How fairy Mab the junkets ate;
She was pinch'd, and pull'd, she said,
And he by friar's lantern led;
Tells how the drudging goblin sweat
To earn his cream-bowl duly set,
When in one night, ere glimpse of morn,
His shadowy flail had thresh'd the corn
That ten day-labourers could not end;
Then lies him down the lubber fiend,
And, stretch'd out all the chimney's length
Basks at the fire his hairy strength;
And crop-full out of doors he flings,
Ere the first cock his matin rings.
  Thus done the tales, to bed they creep,
By whispering winds soon lull'd asleep.
  Tower'd cities please us then
And the busy hum of men,

Where throngs of knights and barons bold,
In weeds of peace high triumphs hold,
With store of ladies, whose bright eyes
Rain influence, and judge the prize
Of wit or arms, while both contend
To win her grace, whom all commend.
There let Hymen oft appear
In saffron robe, with taper clear,
And pomp, and feast, and revelry,
With mask, and antique pageantry;
Such sights as youthful poets dream
On summer eves by haunted stream.
Then to the well-trod stage anon,
If Jonson's learned sock be on,
Or sweetest Shakspeare, Fancy's child,
Warble his native wood-notes wild.
    And ever against eating cares
Lap me in soft Lydian airs
Married to immortal verse,
Such as the meeting soul may pierce
In notes, with many a winding bout
Of linkéd sweetness long drawn out,
With wanton heed and giddy cunning,
The melting voice through mazes running,
Untwisting all the chains that tie
The hidden soul of harmony;
That Orpheus' self may heave his head
From golden slumber, on a bed
Of heap'd Elysian flowers, and hear
Such strains as would have won the ear
Of Pluto, to have quite set free
His half-regain'd Eurydice.
    These delights if thou canst give,
Mirth, with thee I mean to live.

J. Milton.

IL PENSEROSO.

HENCE vain deluding joys,
The brood of Folly, without father bred!
How little you bestead,
    Or fill the fixed mind with all your toys!
Dwell in some idle brain,
And fancies fond with gaudy shapes possess,
As thick and numberless
    As the gay motes that people the sunbeams,
Or likest hov'ring dreams,
    The fickle pensioners of Morpheus' train.
  But hail, thou Goddess, sage and holy!
Hail divinest Melancholy!
Whose saintly visage is too bright
To hit the sense of human sight,
And therefore to our weaker view
O'erlaid with black, staid Wisdom's hue:
Black, but such as in esteem
Prince Memnon's sister might beseem,
Or that starr'd Ethiop queen, that strove
To set her beauty's praise above
The sea-nymphs, and their pow'rs offended,
Yet thou art higher far descended;
Thee bright-hair'd Vesta long of yore
To solitary Saturn bore;
His daughter she (in Saturn's reign
Such mixture was not held a stain).
Oft in glim'ring bow'rs and glades
He met her, and in secret shades

Of woody Ida's inmost grove,
While yet there was no fear of Jove.
 Come, pensive nun, devout and pure,
Sober, steadfast, and demure,
All in a robe of darkest grain
Flowing with majestic train,
And sable stole of cypress lawn,
Over thy decent shoulders drawn.
Come, but keep thy wonted state,
With even step and musing gait,
And looks commercing with the skies,
Thy rapt soul sitting in thine eyes:
There, held in holy passion still,
Forget thyself to marble, till
With a sad leaden downward cast,
Thou fix them on the earth as fast;
And join with thee calm Peace, and Quiet,
Spare Fast, that oft with Gods doth diet,
And hear the Muses in a ring
Aye round about Jove's altar sing;
And add to these retired Leisure,
That in trim gardens takes his pleasure;
But first and chiefest with thee bring
Him that yon soars on golden wing,
Guiding the fiery-wheelèd throne,
The cherub Contemplation;
And the mute Silence hist along,
'Less Philomel will deign a song,
In his sweetest, saddest plight,
Smoothing the rugged brow of Night,
While Cynthia checks her dragon yoke,
Gently o'er th' accustom'd oak;
Sweet bird, that shunn'st the noise of folly,
Most musical, most melancholy!
Thee, chantress, oft the woods among,
I woo to hear thy ev'ning song;

And missing thee, I walk unseen
On the dry smooth-shaven green,
To behold the wand'ring Moon,
Riding near her highest noon,
Like one that had been led astray
Through the Heav'ns' wide pathless way;
And oft, as if her head she bow'd,
Stooping through a fleecy cloud.
 Oft on a plat of rising ground
I hear the far-off curfew sound,
Over some wide-water'd shore
Swinging slow with sullen roar.
 Or if the air will not permit,
Some still, removèd place will fit,
Where glowing embers through the room
Teach light to counterfeit a gloom;
Far from all resort of mirth,
Save the cricket on the hearth,
Or the belman's drowsy charm
To bless the doors from nightly harm.
 Or let my lamp at midnight hour
Be seen in some high lonely tower,
Where I may oft out-watch the Bear
With thrice-great Hermes, or unsphere
The spirit of Plato, to unfold
What worlds or what vast regions hold
The immortal mind, that hath forsook
Her mansion in this fleshly nook:
And of those demons that are found
In fire, air, flood, or under ground,
Whose power hath a true consent
With planet, or with element.
Sometime let gorgeous Tragedy
In scepter'd pall come sweeping by,
Presenting Thebes, or Pelops' line,
Or the tale of Troy divine;

Or what (though rare) of later age
Ennobled hath the buskin'd stage.
   But, O sad Virgin, that thy power
Might raise Musaeus from his bower,
Or bid the soul of Orpheus sing
Such notes as, warbled to the string,
Drew iron tears down Pluto's cheek
And made Hell grant what Love did seek!
Or call up him that left half-told
The story of Cambuscan bold,
Of Camball, and of Algarsife,
And who had Canacé to wife
That own'd the virtuous ring and glass;
And of the wondrous horse of brass
On which the Tartar king did ride;
And if aught else great bards beside
In sage and solemn tunes have sung,
Of tourneys and of trophies hung;
Of forests and enchantments drear,
Where more is meant than meets the ear.
   Thus Night oft see me in thy pale career,
Till civil-suited Morn appear,
Not trick'd and frounc'd as she was wont
With the Attic Boy to hunt,
But kerchief'd in a comely cloud,
While rocking winds are piping loud,
Or usher'd with a shower still,
When the gust hath blown his fill,
Ending on the rustling leaves,
With minute drops from off the eaves.
   And when the sun begins to fling
His flaring beams, me, Goddess, bring
To archèd walks of twilight groves,
And shadows brown, that Sylvan loves,
Of pine or monumental oak,
Where the rude axe with heavèd stroke

Was never heard, the Nymphs to daunt,
Or fright them from their hallow'd haunt.
There in close covert by some brook,
Where no profaner eye may look,
Hide me from day's garish eye,
While the bee with honey'd thigh,
That at her flow'ry work doth sing,
And the waters murmuring,
With such concert as they keep
Entice the dewy-feather'd Sleep;
And let some strange mysterious dream
Wave at his wings in aery stream
Of lively portraiture display'd,
Softly on my eyelids laid:
And as I wake, sweet music breathe
Above, about, or underneath,
Sent by some spirit to mortals good,
Or th' unseen Genius of the wood.
  But let my due feet never fail
To walk the studious cloister's pale,
And love the high-embowéd roof,
With antique pillars massy proof,
And storied windows richly dight
Casting a dim religious light:
There let the pealing organ blow
To the full-voiced quire below
In service high and anthems clear,
As may with sweetness, through mine ear,
Dissolve me into ecstasies,
And bring all Heaven before mine eyes.
  And may at last my weary age
Find out the peaceful hermitage,
The hairy gown and mossy cell
Where I may sit and rightly spell
Of every star that heaven doth show,
And every herb that sips the dew;

Till old experience do attain
To something like prophetic strain.
  These pleasures, Melancholy, give,
And I with thee will choose to live.

J. Milton.

ON MELANCHOLY.

1.

WHEN I go musing all alone,
Thinking of divers things foreknown;
When I build castles in the air,
Void of sorrow, void of care,
Pleasing myself with phantasms sweet,
Methinks the time runs very fleet.
    All my joys to this are folly;
    Naught so sweet as melancholy!

2.

When I go walking all alone,
Recounting what I have ill-done,
My thoughts on me then tyrannise,
Fear and sorrow me surprise,
Whether I tarry still, or go,
Methinks the time moves very slow.
    All my griefs to this are jolly;
    Naught so sad as melancholy.

3.

When to myself I act and smile,
With pleasing thoughts the time beguile,
By a brookside or wood so green,
Unheard, unsought for, or unseen,
A thousand pleasures do me bless,
And crown my soul with happiness.
    All my joys besides are folly;
    None so sweet as melancholy.

4.

When I lie, sit, or walk alone,
I sigh, I grieve, making great moan;
In a dark grove or irksome den,
With discontents and furies then,
A thousand miseries at once
Mine heavy heart and soul ensconce.
  All my griefs to this are jolly;
  None so sour as melancholy.

5.

Methinks I hear, methinks I see
Sweet music, wondrous melody,
Towns, palaces and cities fine;
Here now, then there, the world is mine;
Rare beauties, gallants, ladies shine,
Whate'ver is lovely, is divine.
  All other joys to this are folly;
  None so sweet as melancholy.

6.

Methinks I hear, methinks I see
Ghosts, goblins, fiends: my fantasy
Presents a thousand ugly shapes;
Headless bears, black men, and apes;
Doleful outcries, fearful sights
My sad and dismal soul affrights.
  All my griefs to this are jolly;
  None so damn'd as melancholy.

Robert Burton.

MELANCOLIA.

HENCE, all you vain delights,
As short as are the nights
Wherein you spend your folly:
There's nought in this life sweet,
If man were wise to see't,
But only melancholy,
O sweetest Melancholy!
Welcome, folded arms, and fixéd eyes,
A sigh that piercing mortifies,
A look that's fasten'd to the ground,
A tongue chain'd up without a sound!
Fountain heads and pathless groves,
Places which pale passion loves!
Moonlight walks, when all the fowls
Are warmly housed, save bats and owls!
A midnight bell, a parting groan!
These are the sounds we feed upon;
Then stretch our bones in a still gloomy valley;
Nothing's so dainty sweet as lovely melancholy.

F. Beaumont.

MEMORY AND MELANCHOLY.

MEMORY, hither come,
　And tune your merry notes:
And while upon the wind
　Your music floats,
I'll pore upon the stream
Where sighing lovers dream,
　And fish for fancies as they pass
　Within the watery glass.

I'll drink of the clear stream,
　And hear the linnet's song,
And then I'll lie and dream
　The day along:
And when night comes, I'll go
To places fit for woe,
　Walking along the darken'd valley
　With silent melancholy.

William Blake.

LOVE AND DEATH.

GLORIES, pleasures, pomps, delights and ease,
      Can but please
The outward senses, when the mind
Is or untroubled, or by peace refined.
Crowns may flourish and decay,
Beauties shine, but fade away.
Youth may revel, yet it must
Lie down in a bed of dust.
Earthly honours flow and waste,
Time alone doth change and last.
Sorrows mingled with contents, prepare
      Rest for care;
Love only reigns in death; though art
Can find no comfort for a broken heart.

John Ford.

SORROW-SONG.

OH, sorrow, sorrow, say where dost thou dwell?
  In the lowest room of hell.
Art thou born of human race?
  No, no, I have a furier face.
Art thou in city, town, or court?
  I to every place resort.
Oh, why into the world is sorrow sent?
  Men afflicted best repent.
What dost thou feed on?
      Broken sleep.
What tak'st thou pleasure in?
      To weep,
      To sigh, to sob, to pine, to groan,
      To wring my hands, to sit alone.
Oh when, oh when shall sorrow quiet have?
  Never, never, never, never.
  Never till she finds a grave.

Samuel Rowley.

SLUMBER-SONG.

CARE-CHARMING Sleep, thou easer of all woes,—
Brother to Death, sweetly thyself dispose
On this afflicted prince; fall like a cloud
In gentle showers; give nothing that is loud
Or painful to his slumbers;—easy, sweet,
And as a purling stream, thou son of Night,
Pass by his troubled senses:—sing his pain
Like hollow murmuring wind, or silver rain.
　　Into this prince gently, oh, gently slide,
　　And kiss him into slumbers like a bride!

John Fletcher.

TO ECHO.

SWEET Echo, sweetest nymph, that liv'st unseen
　　Within thy aery shell,
　By slow Meander's margent green,
And in the violet-embroider'd vale,
　　Where the love-lorn nightingale
Nightly to thee her sad song mourneth well;
Canst thou not tell me of a gentle pair
　　That likest thy Narcissus are?
　　O, if thou have
Hid them in some flowery cave,
　　Tell me but where,
　Sweet queen of parley, daughter of the sphere!
　So may'st thou be translated to the skies,
And give resounding grace to all Heaven's harmonies.

J. Milton.

ORPHEUS.

ORPHEUS with his lute made trees,
And the mountain-tops that freeze,
  Bow themselves when he did sing.
To his music plants and flowers
Ever sprung; as sun and showers
  There had made a lasting spring.

Everything that heard him play,
Even the billows of the sea,
  Hung their heads and then lay by.
In sweet music is such art,
Killing Care and Grief of Heart
  Fall asleep, or hearing, die!

W. Shakespeare.

PRAISE OF MUSIC.

When whispering strains do softly steal
  With creeping passion through the heart,
And when at ev'ry touch we feel
  Our pulses beat and bear a part;
    When threads can make
    A heart-string quake,
    Philosophy
    Can scarce deny
The soul consists of harmony.

O lull me, lull me, charming air,
  My sense is rock'd with wonder sweet!
Like snow on wool thy fallings are—
  Soft like a spirit's are thy feet.
    Grief who need fear
    That hath an ear?
    Down let him lie,
    And slumb'ring die,
And change his soul for harmony.

William Strode.

A BRIDAL SONG.

ROSES, their sharp spines being gone,
Not royal in their smells alone,
   But in their hue;
Maiden-pinks, of odour faint,
Daisies smell-less, yet most quaint,
   And sweet thyme true;

Primrose, first-born child of Ver,
Merry spring-time's harbinger,
   With her bells dim;
Oxlips in their cradles growing,
Marigolds on death-beds blowing,
   Lark-heels trim.

All, dear Nature's children sweet,
Lie 'fore bride and bridegroom's feet,
   Blessing their sense!
Not an angel of the air,
Bird melodious, or bird fair,
   Be absent hence!

The crow, the slanderous cuckoo, nor
The boding raven, nor chough hoar,
   Nor chattering pie,
May on our bride-house perch or sing,
Or with them any discord bring,
   But from it fly!

F. Beaumont.

A FOREST-DITTY.

UNDER the greenwood tree
Who loves to lie with me,
And tune his merry note
Unto the sweet bird's throat,
Come hither, come hither, come hither;
Here shall he see
No enemy,
But winter and rough weather.

Who doth ambition shun,
And loves to lie i' the sun,
Seeking the food he eats,
And pleas'd with what he gets,
Come hither, come hither, come hither;
Here shall he see
No enemy,
But winter and rough weather.

W. Shakespeare.

ARCHERS THREE.

WE three Archers be,
Rangers that rove through the north countree,
Lovers of ven'son and liberty,
  That value not honours or money.

We three good fellows be,
That never yet ran from three times three.
Quarterstaff, broadsword, or bowmanry,
  But give us fair play for our money.

We three merry men be,
At a lass or a glass under greenwood tree;
Jocundly chaunting our ancient glee,
  Though we had not a penny of money.

Anonymous.

TO DIANA.

HAIL, beauteous Dian, queen of shades,
That dwell'st beneath these shadowy glades,
Mistress of all those beauteous maids
    That are by her allowed.
Virginity we all profess,
Abjure the worldly vain excess,
And will to Dian yield no less
    Than we to her have vowed.
The shepherds, satyrs, nymphs, and fawns,
For thee will trip it o'er the lawns.

Come, to the forest let us go,
And trip it like the barren doe;
The fawns and satyrs still do so,
    And freely thus they may.
The fairies dance and satyrs sing,
And on the grass tread many a ring,
And to their caves their ven'son bring;
    And we will do as they.
        The shepherds, satyrs, &c., &c.

Our food is honey from the bees,
And mellow fruits that drop from trees;
In chace we climb the high degrees
    Of every steepy mountain.
And when the weary day is past,
We at the evening hie us fast,
And after this, our field repast,
    We drink the pleasant fountain.
        The shepherds, satyrs, &c., &c.

Thomas Heywood.

7*

INVOCATION TO DIANA.

QUEEN and huntress, chaste and fair,
Now the sun is laid to sleep,
Seated in thy silver chair,
State in wonted manner keep.
  Hesperus entreats thy light,
  Goddess excellently bright!

Earth, let not thy envious shade
Dare itself to interpose;
Cynthia's shining orb was made
Heaven to clear, when day did close.
  Bless us then with wishéd sight,
  Goddess excellently bright!

Lay thy bow of pearl apart,
And thy crystal-shining quiver:
Give unto the flying hart
Space to breathe how short soever;
  Thou that mak'st a day of night,
  Goddess excellently bright!

B. Jonson.

TO APOLLO.

SING to Apollo, god of day,
Whose golden beams with morning play,
And make her eyes so brightly shine,
Aurora's face is called divine.
Sing to Phœbus and that throne
Of diamonds which he sets upon.
    Io Pæans let us sing
    To Physic and to Poesy's king.

Crown all his altars with bright fire,
Laurels bind about his lyre,
A Daphnean coronet for his head,
The Muses dance about his bed;
When on his ravishing lute he plays,
Strew his temple round with bays.
    Io Pæans let us sing
    To the glittering Delian king.

J. Lylye.

TO BACCHUS.

TO BACCHUS.

GOD Lyæus ever young,
Ever renowned, ever sung,
Stain'd with blood of lusty grapes
In a thousand lusty shapes;
Dance upon the mazer's brim;
In the crimson liquor swim!
From thy plenteous hand divine
Let a river run with wine!

F. Beaumont.

DANCING CHORUS.

SHAKE off your heavy trance,
And leap into a dance
    Such as no mortals use to tread;
Fit only for Apollo
    To play to, for the moon to lead,
And all the stars to follow!

F. Beaumont.

HOLIDAY IN ARCADIA.

WOODMEN, shepherds, come away,
This is Pan's great holiday,
   Throw off cares,
With your heaven-aspiring airs
   Help us to sing,
While valleys with your echoes ring.

Nymphs that dwell within these groves,
Leave your arbours, bring your loves,
   Gather posies,
Crown your golden hair with roses;
   As you pass
Foot like fairies on the grass.

Joy crown our bowers! Philomel,
Leave of Tereus' rape to tell.
   Let trees dance,
As they at Thracian lyre did once;
   Mountains play,
This is the shepherds' holiday.

J. Shirley.

SONG OF A SATYR.

THROUGH yon same bending plain
That flings his arms down to the main,
And through these thick woods, have I run,
Whose bottom never kissed the sun
Since the lusty spring began;
All to please my Master Pan,
Have I trotted without rest
To get him fruit; for at a feast
He entertains, this coming night,
His paramour, the Syrinx bright.
   *   *   *   *
Here be grapes, whose lusty blood
Is the learnèd poet's good;
Sweeter yet did never crown
The head of Bacchus! nuts more brown
Than the squirrel's teeth that crack them;
Deign, oh fairest fair, to take them!
For these black-eyèd Dryope
Hath often-times commanded me
With my claspèd knee to climb:
See how well the lusty time
Hath decked their rising cheeks in red,
Such as on your lips is spread!
Here be berries for a queen,
Some be red, some be green;
These are of that luscious meat,
The great god Pan himself doth eat:
All these, and what the woods can yield,
The hanging mountain, or the field,

I freely offer, and ere long
Will bring you more, more sweet and strong;
Till when, humbly leave I take,
Lest the great Pan do awake,
That sleeping lies in a deep glade,
Under a broad beech's shade.
I must go, I must run
Swifter than the fiery sun.

J. Fletcher.

EVENSONG.

SHEPHERDS all, and maidens fair,
Fold your flocks up, for the air
'Gins to thicken, and the sun
Already his great course hath run.
See the dew-drops how they kiss
Every little flower that is,
Hanging on their velvet heads,
Like a rope of crystal beads:
See the heavy clouds low falling,
And bright Hesperus down calling
The dead Night from under ground;
At whose rising, mists unsound,
Damps and vapours fly apace,
Hovering o'er the wanton face
Of these pastures, where they come,
Striking dead both bud and bloom:
Therefore, from such danger lock
Every one his lovèd flock;
And let your dogs lie loose without,
Lest the wolf come as a scout
From the mountain, and, ere day,
Bear a lamb or kid away;

Or the crafty thievish fox
Break upon your simple flocks.
To secure yourselves from these,
Be not too secure in ease;
Let one eye his watches keep,
Whilst the other eye doth sleep;
So you shall good shepherds prove,
And for ever hold the love
Of our great god. Sweetest slumbers,
And soft silence, fall in numbers
On your eye-lids! So, farewell!
Thus I end my evening's knell.

J. Fletcher.

MATIN-SONG.

HARK! hark! the lark at heaven's gate sings,
    And Phœbus 'gins arise,
His steeds to water at those springs
    On chalic'd flowers that lies;
And winking Mary-buds begin
    To ope their golden eyes,
With every thing that pretty bin;--
    My lady sweet, arise!

W. Shakespeare.

DAWN-SONG.

THE lark now leaves his watery nest
    And, climbing, shakes his dewy wings,
He takes this window for the East,
    And to implore your light, he sings.
        Awake! awake! the morn will never rise
        Till she can dress her beauty at your eyes.

The merchant bows unto the seaman's star;
    The ploughman from the sun his season takes;
But still the lover wonders what they are
    Who look for day before his mistress wakes.
        Awake! awake! break through your veils of lawn!
        Then draw your curtains, and begin the dawn.

Sir William Davenant.

GOOD-MORROW.

PACK clouds away, and welcome day,
  With night we banish sorrow;
Sweet air, blow soft; mount, larks, aloft,
  To give my love good-morrow.
Wings from the wind to please her mind,
  Notes from the lark I'll borrow;
Bird, prune thy wing; nightingale, sing,
  To give my love good-morrow.

Wake from thy nest, robin redbreast;
  Sing, birds, in every furrow;
And from each hill let music shrill
  Give my fair love good-morrow.
Blackbird and thrush in every bush,
  Stare, linnet, and cock-sparrow;
You pretty elves, among yourselves
  Sing my fair love good-morrow.

T. Heywood.

SERENADE TO SYLVIA.

WHO is Sylvia? what is she,
  That all our swains commend her?
Holy, fair, and wise is she;
  The heavens such grace did lend her,
That she might admiréd be.

Is she kind, as she is fair?
  For beauty lives with kindness;
Love doth to her eyes repair,
  To help him of his blindness;
And, being helped, inhabits there.

Then to Sylvia let us sing,
  That Sylvia is excelling;
She excels each mortal thing
  Upon the dull earth dwelling:
To her let us garlands bring.

W. Shakespeare.

SERENADE TO JULIA.

HER eyes the glow-worm lend thee,
The shooting stars attend thee;
    And the elves also,
    Whose little eyes glow
Like the sparks of fire, befriend thee!

No Will-o'-the-wisp mislight thee,
Nor snake or slow-worm bite thee!
    But on, on thy way,
    Not making a stay,
Since ghost there is none to affright thee.

Let not the dark thee cumber;
What though the moon does slumber?
    The stars of the night
    Will lend thee their light,
Like tapers clear without number.

Then Julia let me woo thee,
Thus, thus to come unto me;
    And, when I shall meet
    Thy silvery feet,
My soul I'll pour into thee.

R. Herrick.

THE LOVER TO THE GLOW-WORMS.

YE living lamps! by whose dear light
  The nightingale doth sit so late,
And, studying all the summer night,
  Her matchless songs doth meditate!

Ye country comets! that portend
  No war, nor prince's funeral,—
Shining unto no other end
  Than to presage the grass's fall!

Ye glow-worms, whose officious flame
  To wandering mowers shows the way,
That in the night have lost their aim,
  And after foolish fires do stray—

Your courteous lights in vain you waste,
  Since Juliana here is come;
For she my mind hath so displaced,
  That I shall never find my home.

A. Marvell.

TO ELIZABETH OF BOHEMIA.

You meaner beauties of the night,
  Which poorly satisfy our eyes
More by your number than your light,
  You common people of the skies,
What are you, when the Moon shall rise?

Ye violets that first appear,
  By your pure purple mantles known
Like the proud virgins of the year
  As if the spring were all your own,—
What are you, when the Rose is blown?

Ye curious chanters of the wood
  That warble forth dame Nature's lays,
Thinking your passions understood
  By your weak accents; what's your praise
When Philomel her voice doth raise?

So when my Mistress shall be seen
  In sweetness of her looks and mind,
By virtue first, then choice, a Queen,
  Tell me, if she were not design'd
Th' eclipse and glory of her kind?

Sir H. Wotton.

THE ROSES IN CASTARA'S BOSOM.

YE blushing virgins happy are
In the chaste nunnery of her breasts,
For he'd profane so chaste a fair,
Who e'er should call them Cupid's nests.

Transplanted thus, how bright ye grow!
How rich a perfume do ye yield!
In some close garden, cowslips so
Are sweeter than i' the open field.

In those white cloisters live secure
From the rude blasts of wanton breath,
Each hour more innocent and pure,
Till you shall wither into death.

Then that which living gave you room,
Your glorious sepulchre shall be.
There wants no marble for a tomb
Whose breast hath marble been to me.

William Habington.

GO, HAPPY ROSE!

Go, happy Rose! and, interwove
With other flowers, bind my love!
  Tell her, too, she must not be
  Longer flowing, longer free,
  That so oft hath fettered me.

Say, if she's fretful, I have bands
Of pearl and gold to bind her hands;
  Tell her, if she struggle still,
  I have myrtle rods at will,
  For to tame, though not to kill.

Take then my blessing thus, and go,
And tell her this,—but do not so!
  Lest a handsome anger fly,
  Like a lightning from her eye.
  And burn thee up, as well as I.

R. Herrick.

THE ROSE'S MESSAGE.

Go, lovely Rose!
Tell her, that wastes her time and me,
  That now she knows,
When I resemble her to thee,
How sweet and fair she seems to be.

Tell her that's young
And shuns to have her graces spied,
  That hadst thou sprung
In deserts, where no men abide,
Thou must have uncommended died.

Small is the worth
Of beauty from the light retired:
  Bid her come forth,
Suffer herself to be desired,
And not blush so to be admired.

Then die! that she
The common fate of all things rare
  May read in thee:
How small a part of time they share
That are so wondrous sweet and fair!

Edmund Waller.

THE LOVER AND THE ROSE.

Go, rose! my Chloe's bosom grace!
　How happy should I prove,
Might I supply that envied place
　With never-fading love:
There, Phœnix-like, beneath her eye,
Involved in fragrance, burn and die!

Know, hapless flower, that thou shalt find
　More fragrant roses there:
I see thy withering head reclined
　With envy and despair.
One common fate we both must prove,—
You die with envy, I with love.

John Gay.

TO ALTHEA—(FROM PRISON).

WHEN Love with unconfinéd wings
  Hovers within my gates,
And my divine Althea brings
  To whisper at the grates;
When I lie tangled in her hair
  And fetter'd to her eye,
The birds that wanton in the air
  Know no such liberty.

When flowing cups run swiftly round
  With no allaying Thames,
Our careless heads with roses crown'd,
  Our hearts with loyal flames;
When thirsty grief in wine we steep,
  When healths and draughts go free—
Fishes that tipple in the deep
  Know no such liberty.

When, linnet-like confinéd, I
  With shriller throat shall sing
The sweetness, mercy, majesty
  And glories of my King;
When I shall voice aloud how good
  He is, how great should be,
Enlargéd winds, that curl the flood,
  Know no such liberty.

Stone walls do not a prison make,
  Nor iron bars a cage;
Minds innocent and quiet take
  That for an hermitage:
If I have freedom in my love
  And in my soul am free,
Angels alone, that soar above,
  Enjoy such liberty.

Colonel Lovelace.

BEAUTY CONCEALED.

Do not conceal thy radiant eyes,
The starlight of serenest skies;
Lest, wanting of their heavenly light,
They turn to Chaos' endless night!

Do not conceal those tresses fair,
The silken snares of thy curl'd hair;
Lest, finding neither gold nor ore,
The curious silk-worm work no more!

Do not conceal those breasts of thine,
More snow-white than the Apennine;
Lest, if there be like snow and frost,
The lily be forever lost!

Do not conceal that fragrant scent,
Thy breath, which to all flowers hath lent
Perfumes; lest it being supprest,
No spices grow in all the East!

Do not conceal thy heavenly voice,
Which makes the hearts of gods rejoice;
Lest, Music hearing no such thing,
The nightingale forget to sing!

Do not conceal, nor yet eclipse,
Thy pearly teeth with coral lips;
Lest that the seas cease to bring forth
Gems which from thee have all their worth!

Do not conceal no beauty, grace,
That's either in thy mind or face;
Lest virtue overcome by vice
Make men believe no Paradise!

Sir Francis Kinaston.

TEARS OF PRICE.

THE dew no more shall weep,
  The primrose's pale cheek to deck
The dew no more shall sleep,
  Nuzzled in the lily's neck:
Much rather would it tremble here,
And leave them both to be thy tear.

Not the soft gold which
  Steals from the amber-weeping tree,
Makes sorrow half so rich,
  As the drops distill'd from thee:
Sorrow's best jewels be in these
Caskets, of which Heaven keeps the keys.

When sorrow would be seen
  In her bright majesty,
For she is a Queen!
  Then is she dress'd by none but thee;
Then, and only then, she wears
Her richest pearls;—I mean thy tears

Not in the evening's eyes
  When they red with weeping are
For the sun that dies,
  Sits Sorrow with a face so fair:
No where but here doth meet,
Sweetness so sad, sadness so sweet.

Richard Crashaw.

SONETTO.

FIRST shall the heav'ns want starry light,
  The seas be robb'd of their waves,
The day want sun, the sun want bright,
  The night want shade, the dead men graves,
The April flow'rs, and leaves, and tree,
Before I false my faith to thee.

First shall the top of highest hill
  By humble plains be overpry'd,
And poets scorn the Muses' quill,
  And fish forsake the water glide,
And Iris lose her colour'd weed,
Before I false thee at thy need.

First direful Hate shall turn to peace,
  And Love relent in deep disdain,
And Death his fatal stroke shall cease,
  And Envy pity every pain,
And Pleasure mourn, and sorrow smile,
Before I talk of any guile.

First Time shall stay his stayless race,
  And Winter bless his brows with corn,
And snow bemoisten July's face,
  And Winter sing, and Summer mourn,
Before my pen, by help of Fame,
Cease to recite thy sacred name!

Thomas Lodge.

THE SILENT LOVER.

PASSIONS are liken'd best to floods and streams,
    The shallow murmur, but the deep are dumb;
So when affections yield discourse, it seems
    The bottom is but shallow whence they come;
They that are rich in words must needs discover
They are but poor in that which makes a lover.

Wrong not, sweet mistress of my heart,
    The merit of true passion,
With thinking that he feels no smart
    That sues for no compassion.

Since if my plaints were not t'approve
    The conquest of thy beauty,
It comes not from defect of love,
    But fear t'exceed my duty.

For knowing that I sue to serve
    A saint of such perfection
As all desire, but none deserve
    A place in her affection,

I rather choose to want relief
    Than venture the revealing;
Where glory recommends the grief,
    Despair disdains the healing.

Silence in love betrays more woe
  Than words, though ne'er so witty;
A beggar that is dumb, you know,
  May challenge double pity.

Then wrong not, dearest to my heart,
  My love for secret passion;
He smarteth most who hides his smart,
  And sues for no compassion.

Sir W. Raleigh.

TO ANTHEA, WHO MAY COMMAND HIM
ANY THING.

BID me to live, and I will live
  Thy Protestant to be:
Or bid me love, and I will give
  A loving heart to thee.

A heart as soft, a heart as kind,
  A heart as sound and free
As in the whole world thou canst find—
  That heart I'll give to thee.

Bid that heart stay, and it will stay,
  To honour thy decree:
Or bid it languish quite away,
  And 't shall do so for thee.

Bid me to weep, and I will weep
  While I have eyes to see:
And having none, yet I will keep
  A heart to weep for thee.

Bid me despair, and I'll despair
  Under that cypress tree:
Or bid me die, and I will dare
  E'en Death, to die for thee.

Thou art my life, my love, my heart,
  The very eyes of me;
And hast command of every part,
  To live and die for thee.

R. Herrick.

LOVE'S UNSELFISHNESS.

PHILLIS, men say that all my vows
  Are to thy fortune paid:
Alas! my heart he little knows,
  Who thinks my love a trade.

Were I of all these woods the lord,
  One berry from thy hand
More real pleasure would afford
  Than all my large command.

My humble love has learned to live
  On what the nicest maid,
Without a conscious blush, may give
  Beneath the myrtle shade.

Sir Charles Sedley.

TO HIS LOVE: ON GOING A JOURNEY.

1.

SWEETEST love, I do not go
    For weariness of thee,
Nor in hope the world can show
    A fitter love for me;
        But since that I
    Must die at last, 'tis best
    Thus to use myself in jest
        By feignèd death to die.

2.

Yesternight the sun went hence,
    And yet is here to-day;
He hath no desire nor sense,
    Nor half so short a way:
        Then fear not me,
    But believe that I shall make
    Hastier journeys, since I take
        More wings and spurs than he.

3.

O how feeble is man's pow'r!
    That, if good fortune fall,
Cannot add another hour,
    Nor a lost hour recall;
        But come bad chance,
    And we join to it our strength,
    And we teach it art and length
        Itself o'er us to advance.

4.

When thou sigh'st thou sigh'st not wind,
    But sigh'st my soul away;
When thou weep'st, unkindly kind,
    My life's blood doth decay.
        It cannot be
    That thou lov'st me as thou say'st
    If in thine my life thou waste,
        Which art the life of me.

5.

Let not thy divining heart
    Forethink me any ill;
Destiny may take thy part
    And may thy fears fulfill;
        But think that we
    Are but laid aside to sleep.
    They who one another keep
        Alive, ne'er parted be!

Dr. John Donne.

TO LUCASTA (ON GOING TO THE WARS).

TELL me not, sweet, I am unkind,—
  That from the nunnery
Of thy chaste breast and quiet mind
  To war and arms I fly.

True, a new mistress now I chase,
  The first foe in the field;
And with a stronger faith embrace
  A sword, a horse, a shield.

Yet this inconstancy is such
  As you, too, shall adore;
I could not love thee, dear, so much,
  Loved I not Honour more.

Colonel Lovelace.

THE BATTLE OF AGINCOURT.

FAIR stood the wind for France
When we our sails advance,
Nor now to prove our chance
    Longer will tarry;
But putting to the main,
At Kaux, the mouth of Seine,
With all his martial train,
    Landed King Harry.

And taking many a fort,
Furnish'd in warlike sort
March'd towards Agincourt
    In happy hour;
Skirmishing day by day
With those that stopp'd his way,
Where the French gen'ral lay
    With all his power.

The Duke of York so dread,
The eager vanward led;
With the main Henry sped,
    Amongst his henchmen.
Excester had the rear,
A braver man not there,
O Lord how hot they were
    On the false Frenchmen!

They now to fight are gone,
Armour on armour shone,
Drum now to drum did groan,
　　To hear, was wonder;
That with cries they make,
The very earth did shake,
Trumpet to trumpet spake,
　　Thunder to thunder.

Well it thine age became,
O noble Erpingham,
Which did the signal aim
　　To our hid forces;
When from a meadow by,
Like a storm suddenly,
The English archery
　　Stuck the French horses.

With Spanish yew so strong,
Arrows a cloth-yard long,
That like to serpents stung
　　Piercing the weather;
None from his fellow starts,
But playing manly parts,
And like true English hearts,
　　Stuck close together.

When down their bows they threw
And forth their bilbows drew
And on the French they flew,
　　Not one was tardy;
Arms were from shoulders setn,
Scalps to the teeth were rent,
Down the French peasants went,—
　　Our men were hardy!

This while our noble king,
His broad sword brandishing,
Down the French host did ding,
      As to o'erwhelm it;
And many a deep wound lent,
His arms with blood besprent
And many a cruel dent
      Bruisèd his helmet.

Glo'ster, that duke so good,
Next of the royal blood,
For famous England stood,
      With his brave brother,
Clarence, in steel so bright,
Though but a maiden knight,
Yet in that furious fight
      Scarce such another.

Warwick in blood did wade,
Oxford the foe invade,
And cruel slaughter made,
      Still as they ran up;
Suffolk his axe did ply,
Beaumont and Willoughby
Bare them right doughtily,
      Ferrers and Fanhope.

Upon Saint Crispin's day
Fought was this noble fray,
Which fame did not delay,
      To England to carry;
O when shall Englishmen
With such acts fill a pen,
Or England breed again
      Such a King Harry?

M. Drayton.

9*

SIR PATRICK SPENCE.

(SCOTTISH BALLAD).

THE king sits in Dunfermline town,
 Drinking the blude-red wine:
"O where will I get a skeely skipper
 To sail this ship o' mine?"

Then up and spake an eldern knight
 Sat at the king's right knee:
"Sir Patrick Spence is the best sailor
 That sails upon the sea."

Our king has written a braid letter
 And sealed it with his hand,
And sent it to Sir Patrick Spence
 Was walking on the sand.

"To Noroway, to Noroway,
 To Noroway o'er the foam,
The king's daughter to Noroway,
 'Tis thou must take her home."

"Be it wind or wet, be it hail or sleet,
 Our ship must sail the foam;
The king's daughter to Noroway,
 'Tis we must bring her home."

They hoisted sail on Monday morn
 With all the speed they may;
They have landed safe in Noroway
 Upon the Wednesday.

They hadna been a week, a week
  In Noroway but twae,
When that the lords of Noroway
  Began aloud to say:

"Ye Scotsmen spend all our king's goud
  And all of our queen's fee."
"Ye lie, ye lie, ye liars loud,
  Full loud I hear ye lie!"

"Make ready, make ready, my merry men all,
  Our good ship sails the morn!"
"Now ever alack! my master dear,
  I fear a deadly storm.

I saw the new moon late yestreen,
  With the old moon in her arm;
And if we gang to sea, master,
  I fear we come to harm."

They hadna sailed upon the sea
  A day but barely three,
When loud and boist'rous blew the wind,
  And gurly grew the sea.

"O where will I get a gude sailor
  To take my helm in hand,
While I go up the tall topmast
  To see if I spy land?"

"O here am I, a sailor gude,
  To take the helm in hand,
While you go up the tall topmast;
  But I fear you'll né'er spy land.

He hadna gane a step, a step,
  A step but barely ane,
When a bolt flew out from our goodly ship
  And the salt sea in it came.

“Go fetch a web o’ the silken cloth,
  And another o’ the twine,
And wap them into our ship’s side,
  And letna the sea come in!”

They fetched a web o’ the silken cloth,
  And another o’ the twine,
And they wapped them into that gude ship’s side,
  But still the sea came in.

O loath, loath were our gude Scots lords
  To wet their cork-heel’d shoon;
But long ere all the play was played
  They wet their hats aboon.

O long, long may their ladies sit
  Wi’ their fans into their hand,
Or ere they see Sir Patrick Spence
  Come sailing to the land!

And long, long may their maidens stand
  Wi’ their gold combs in their hair,
Awaiting for their ain dear loves,
  For them they’ll see nae mair.

Have o’er, have o’er to Aberdour!
  ’Tis fifty fathoms deep;
And there lies gude Sir Patrick Spence
  Wi’ the Scots lords at his feet.

Anonymous.

BURD HELEN.

I wish I were where Helen lies;
Night and day on me she cries;
O that I were where Helen lies
    On fair Kirconnell lea!

Curst be the heart that thought the thought,
And curst the hand that fired the shot,
When in my arms burd Helen dropt,
    And died to succour me!

O think na but my heart was sair
When my Love dropt down and spak nae mair!
I laid her down wi' meikle care
    On fair Kirconnell lea.

As I went down the water-side,
None but my foe to be my guide,
None but my foe to be my guide,
    On fair Kirconnell lea;

I lighted down my sword to draw,
I hackéd him in pieces sma',
I hackéd him in pieces sma',
    For her sake that died for me.

O Helen fair, beyond compare!
I'll make a garland of thy hair,
Shall bind my heart for evermair,
    Until the day I die.

O that I were where Helen lies!
Night and day on me she cries;
Out of my bed she bids me rise,
    Says, "Haste, and come to me!"

O Helen fair! O Helen chaste!
If I were with thee, I were blest,
Where thou lies low, and takes thy rest,
    On fair Kirconnell Lee.

I wish my grave were growing green,
A winding sheet drawn ouer my een,
And I in Helen's arms lying,
    On fair Kirconnell Lee.

I wish I were where Helen lies!
Night and day on me she cries;
And I am weary of the skies,
    For her sake that died for me.

Anonymous.

EDWARD OF THE BLOODY BRAND.

"WHY does your brand so drop with blood?
    Edward! Edward!
Why does your brand so drop with blood,
  And why so sad go ye, O?"

"O! I have killed my hawk so good,
        Mother! Mother!
O! I have killed my hawk so good,
  And I have no more but he, O!"

"Your hawk's blood was never so red,
        Edward! Edward!
Your hawk's blood was never so red,
  My dear son, I tell thee, O!"

"O! I have killed my red roan steed,
        Mother! Mother!
O! I have killed my red roan steed,
  That once was fair and free, O!"

"Your steed was old and ye have got more,
        Edward! Edward!
Your steed was old and ye have got more,
  Some other dule you drie, O!"

"O! I have killed my father dear,
    Mother! Mother!
O! I have killed my father dear,
 Alas, and woe is me, O!"

"And what penance will ye drie for that?
    Edward! Edward!
And what penance will ye drie for that?
 My dear son, now tell me, O!"

"I'll set my feet in yonder boat,
    Mother! Mother!
I'll set my feet in yonder boat,
 And I'll fare over the sea, O!"

"And what will you do with your towers and your hall?
    Edward! Edward!
And what will you do with your towers and your hall,
 That were so fair to see, O?"

"I'll let them stand till they down fall,
    Mother! Mother!
I'll let them stand till they down fall,
 For here never more must I be, O!"

"And what will you leave to your bairns and your wife?
    Edward! Edward!
And what will you leave to your bairns and your wife,
When you go over the sea, O?"

"The world's room, let them beg through life,
    Mother! Mother!
The world's room, let them beg through life,
 For them never more will I see, O!"

"And what will you leave to your own mother dear?
    Edward! Edward!
And what will you leave to your own mother dear?
  My dear son, now tell me, O!"

"The curse of hell from me shall you bear,
    Mother! Mother!
The curse of hell from me shall you bear,
  Such counsels you gave to me, O!"

Sir David Dalrymple (Lord Hailes).

A SONG OF INDIFFERENCE.

BLOW, blow, thou winter wind,
Thou art not so unkind
As man's ingratitude;
Thy tooth is not so keen
Because thou art not seen,
Although thy breath be rude.
Heigh ho! sing heigh ho! unto the green holly:
Most friendship is feigning, most loving mere folly:
Then, heigh ho! the holly!
This life is most jolly.

Freeze, freeze, thou bitter sky,
Thou dost not bite so nigh
As benefits forgot:
Though thou the waters warp,
Thy sting is not so sharp
As friend remember'd not.
Heigh ho! sing heigh ho! unto the green holly:
Most friendship is feigning, most loving mere folly:
Then, heigh ho! the holly!
This life is most jolly.

W. Shakespeare.

ALL OR NONE.

SHALL I like a hermit dwell,
On a rock or in a cell,
Calling home the smallest part
That is missing of my heart,
To bestow it where I may
Meet a rival every day?
    If she undervalue me,
    What care I how fair she be?

Were her tresses angel-gold,
If a stranger may be bold,
Unrebuked, unafraid,
To convert them to a braid;
And with little more ado
Work them into bracelets, too;
    If the mine be grown so free,
    What care I how rich it be?

Were her hands as rich a prize
As her hairs or precious eyes;
If she lay them out to take
Kisses for good manners' sake;
And let every lover skip
From her hand unto her lip;
    If she be not chaste to me,
    What care I how chaste she be?

No; she must be perfect snow,
In effect as well as show,
Warming but as snow-balls do,
Not like fire, by burning too;
But when she by change hath got
To her heart a second lot;
    Then, if others share with me,
    Farewell her, whate'er she be!

Sir W. Raleigh.

LOVE'S REQUIREMENTS.

SHALL I, wasting in despair,
Die because a woman's fair?
Or make pale my cheeks with care
'Cause another's rosy are?
Be she fairer than the day,
Or the flow'ry meads in May,
    If she be not so to me,
    What care I how fair she be?

Should my heart be griev'd or pin'd
'Cause I see a woman kind?
Or a well-disposèd nature
Joinèd with a lovely feature?
Be she meeker, kinder than
Turtle-dove or pelican,
    If she be not so to me,
    What care I how kind she be?

Shall a woman's virtues move
Me to perish for her love?
Or her well-deservings, known,
Make me quite forget my own?
Be she with that goodness blest
Which may gain her name of best,
　If she be not such to me,
　What care I how good she be?

'Cause her fortune seems too high,
Shall I play the fool and die?
Those that bear a noble mind,
Where they want of riches find,
Think what with them they would do
That without them dare to woo;
　And unless that mind I see,
　What care I how great she be?

Great, or good, or kind, or fair,
I will ne'er the more despair:
If she love me, this believe,
I will die ere she shall grieve:
If she slight me when I woo,
I can scorn and let her go;
　For if she be not for me,
　What care I for whom she be?

George Wither.

LOVE, LOVE'S DUE.

AWAY with these self-loving lads
Whom Cupid's arrow never glads!
Away, poor souls, that sigh and weep,
In love of them that lie and sleep!
    For Cupid is a merry god,
    And forceth none to kiss the rod.

Sweet Cupid's shafts, like destiny,
Do causeless good or ill decree:
Desert is borne out of his bow,
Reward upon his wing doth go.
    What fools are they that have not known
    That love likes no laws but his own!

My songs, they be of Cynthia's praise:
I wear her rings on holy-days;
On every tree I write her name,
And every day I read the same.
    Where Honor Cupid's rival is,
    There miracles are seen of his.

If Cynthia crave her ring of me,
I blot her name out of the tree.
If doubt do darken things held dear,
Then well-fare nothing once a year.
  For many run, but one must win:
  Fools only hedge the cuckoo in.

The worth that worthiness should move
Is love, which is the due of love;
And love as well the shepherd can
As can the mighty nobleman.
  Sweet nymph, 'tis true, you worthy be;
  Yet, without love, naught worth to me.
Fulke Greville, Lord Brooke.

THE BOLDNESS OF HUMILITY.

By Heaven! I'll tell her boldly that 't is she!
　Why should she shamed or angry be
　　To be beloved by me?
　The gods may give their altars o'er,—
　They'll smoke but seldom any more,
If none but happy men must them adore.

The lightning, which tall oaks oppose in vain,
　To strike sometimes does not disdain
　The humble furzes of the plain.
　She being so high, and I so low,
　Her power by this does greater show,
Who at such distance gives so sure a blow.

Compared with her all things so worthless prove,
　That naught on earth can toward her move,
　Till 't be exalted by her love.
　Equal to her, alas! there's none;
　She like a deity is grown,
That must create, or else must be alone.

If there be man who thinks himself so high
　As to pretend equality,
　He deserves her less than I;
　For he would cheat for his relief,
　And one would give with lesser grief
To an undeserving beggar than a thief.

A. Cowley

SWEET-AND-TWENTY.

O MISTRESS mine, where are you roaming?
O, stay and hear; your true love's coming,
　That can sing both high and low.
Trip no further, pretty sweeting;
Journeys end in lovers' meeting,
　Every wise man's son doth know.

What is love? 'tis not hereafter;
Present mirth hath present laughter;
　What's to come is still unsure:
In delay there lies no plenty;
Then come kiss me, sweet-and-twenty,
　Youth's a stuff will not endure.

W. Shakespeare.

COUNSEL TO GIRLS.

GATHER ye rose-buds while ye may,
  Old Time is still a-flying:
And this same flower that smiles to-day,
  To-morrow will be dying.

The glorious Lamp of Heaven, the Sun,
  The higher he's a getting
The sooner will his race be run,
  And nearer he's to setting.

That age is best which is the first,
  When youth and blood are warmer;
But being spent, the worse, and worst
  Times, still succeed the former.

Then be not coy, but use your time;
  And while ye may, go marry:
For having lost but once your prime,
  You may for ever tarry.

R. Herrick.

FAIR AND FALSE.

IF thou beest born to strange sights,
  Things invisible to see,
Ride ten thousand days and nights
  Till age snow white hairs on thee;
Thou, when thou return'st wilt tell me
All strange wonders that befell thee,
        And swear,
        No where,
    Lives a woman true and fair.

If thou find one, let me know,
  Such a pilgrimage were sweet;—
Yet do not! I would not go,
  Though at next door we might meet.
Though she were true when you met her,
And lasted till you wrote your letter,
        Yet she,
        Will be,
    False ere I come, to two or three!

Dr. J. Donne.

ADVICE TO A LOVER.

WHY so pale and wan, fond lover?
    Prithee, why so pale?
Will, when looking well can't move her,
    Looking ill prevail?
    Prithee, why so pale?

Why so dull and mute, young sinner?
    Prithee, why so mute?
Will, when speaking well can't win her,
    Saying nothing do't?
    Prithee, why so mute?

Quit, quit, for shame! this will not move,
    This cannot take her.
If of herself she will not love,
    Nothing can make her.
    The devil take her!

Sir John Suckling.

LOVE OR DISDAIN.

GIVE me more love, or more disdain;
　The torrid or the frozen zone
Brings equal ease unto my pain;
　The temperate affords me none:
Either extreme, of love or hate,
　Is sweeter than a calm estate.

Give me a storm; if it be love—
　Like Danaë in a golden shower,
I swim in pleasure; if it prove
　Disdain, that torrent will devour
My vulture hopes; and he's possess'd
　Of heaven, that's but from hell releas'd.
Then crown my joys, or cure my pain;
Give me more love, or more disdain.

T. Carew.

LITTLE BUT LONG.

LOVE me little, love me long,
Is the burden of my song.
Love that is too hot and strong
    Burneth soon to waste.
Still I would not have thee cold,
Not too backward or too bold;
Love that lasteth till 'tis old
    Fadeth not in haste.

If thou lovest me too much,
It will not prove as true as touch;
Love me little, more than such,
    For I fear the end.
I am with little well content,
And a little from thee sent
Is enough, with true intent,
    To be steadfast, friend.

Say thou lov'st me while thou live,
I to thee my love will give,
Never dreaming to deceive
    While that life endures:
Nay, and after death, in sooth,
I to thee will keep my truth,
As now, when in my May of youth,
    This my love assures.

Constant love is moderate ever,
And it will through life persever;
Give me that—with true endeavour
    I will it restore.
A suit of durance let it be,
For all weathers; that for me,
For the land or for the sea,
    Lasting evermore.

Winter's cold or summer's heat,
Autumn's tempests on it beat,
It can never know defeat,
    Never can rebel.
Such the love that I would gain,
Such the love, I tell thee plain,
Thou must give, or woo in vain;
    So to thee farewell.

Anonymous (1570).

LOVE BROOKS NO RIVAL.

My dear and only love, I pray
  That little world of thee
Be governed by no other sway
  But purest monarchy;
For if confusion have a part,
  Which virtuous souls abhor,
I'll call a synod in my heart,
  And never love thee more.

As Alexander I will reign,
  And I will reign alone;
My thoughts did evermore disdain
  A rival on my throne.
He either fears his fate too much,
  Or his deserts are small,
Who dares not put it to the touch,
  To gain or lose it all.

But I will reign and govern still,
  And always give the law,
And have each subject at my will,
  And all to stand in awe;
But 'gainst my batteries if I find
  Thou storm or vex me sore,
As if thou set me as a blind,
  I'll never love thee more.

And in the empire of thy heart,
　Where I should solely be,
If others do pretend a part,
　Or dare to share with me;
Or committees if thou erect,
　Or go on such a score—
I'll smiling mock at thy neglect,
　And never love thee more.

But if no faithless action stain
　Thy love and constant word,
I'll make thee famous by my pen,
　And glorious by my sword;
I'll serve thee in such noble ways
　As ne'er was known before;
I'll deck and crown thy head with bays,
　And love thee more and more.

James Grahame, Marquis of Montrose.

LOVE'S SEMBLANCE.

"WHEN Love was first begot,
  And by the mover's will
Did fall to humane lot
  His solace to fulfill,
Devoid of all deceipt,
  A chast and holy fire
Did quicken man's conceipt,
  And women's brest inspire;
The Gods that saw the good
  That mortals did approve
With kind and holy mood,
  Began to talke of Love.

But during this accord,
  A wonder strange to heare;
Whilest Love in deed and word
  Most faythfull did appeare,
False semblance came in place,
  By jealousie attended,
And with a double face
  Both love and fancie blended;
Which make the Gods forsake,
  And men from fancie flie,
And maidens' scorne a make,
  Forsooth, and so will I."

T. Lodge.

THE NOBLER LOVE.

ADIEU, fond love! Farewell, you wanton powers!
      I am free again.
Thou dull disease of bloud and idle hours,
      Bewitching pain,
  Fly to fools, that sigh away their time:
  My nobler love to heaven doth climb,
And there behold beauty still young,
    That time can ne'er corrupt, nor death destroy,
Immortal sweetness by fair angels sung,
    And honoured by eternity and joy:
There lies my love; thither my hopes aspire;
Fond love declines—this heavenly love grows higher.

Beaumont and Fletcher.

THE POETRY OF DRESS.

A SWEET disorder in the dress
Kindles in clothes a wantonness:—
A lawn about the shoulders thrown
Into a fine distractión,—
An erring lace, which here and there
Enthrals the crimson stomacher,—
A cuff neglectful, and thereby
Ribbands to flow confusedly,—
A winning wave, deserving note,
In the tempestuous petticoat,—
A careless shoe-string, in whose tie
I see a wild civility,—
Do more bewitch me, then when art
Is too precise in every part.

R. Herrick.

THE SWEET NEGLECT.

STILL to be neat, still to be drest,
As you were going to a feast:
Still to be poud'red, still perfum'd:
Lady, it is to be presum'd,
Though art's hid causes are not found,
All is not sweet, all is not sound.

Give me a looke, give me a face,   .
That makes simplicitie a grace;
Robes loosely flowing, haire as free:
Such sweet neglect more taketh me
Than all th' adulteries of art
That strike mine eyes, but not my heart.

B. Jonson.

ON A GIRDLE.

THAT which her slender waist confined
Shall now my joyful temples bind:
No monarch but would give his crown,
His arms might do what this has done.
It was my heaven's extremest sphere,
The pale which held that lovely dear.
My joy, my grief, my hope, my love,
Did all within this circle move!—
A narrow compass! and yet there
Dwelt all that's good, and all that's fair.
Give me but what this ribbon bound;
Take all the rest the sun goes round.

E. Waller.

TO DAFFODILS.

FAIR daffodils, we weep to see
  You haste away so soon;
As yet the early rising sun
  Has not attained his noon.
      Stay, stay,
    Until the hasting day
      Has run
    But to the even-song!
And, having prayed together, we
  Will go with you along.

We have short time to stay as you,
  We have as short a spring,
As quick a breath to meet decay,
  As you, or any thing.
      We die
    As your hours do, and dry
      Away,
    Like to the summer's rain,
Or as the pearls of morning dew,
  Ne'er to be found again.

R. Herrick.

LIFE AND THE FLOWERS.

I MADE a posy while the day ran by:
"Here will I smell my remnant out, and tie
My life within this band."

But Time did beckon to the flowers, and they
By noon most cunningly did steal away,
And withered in my hand.

My hand was next to them, and then my heart.
I took, without more thinking, in good part
Time's gentle admonition;

Who did so sweetly death's sad taste convey,
Making my mind to smell my fatal day,
Yet sugaring the suspicion.

Farewell, dear flow'rs! sweetly your time ye spent;
Fit, while ye lived, for smell or ornament;
And after death, for cures.

I follow straight, without complaints or grief;
Since, if my scent be good, I care not if
It be as short as yours.

G. Herbert.

TO BLOSSOMS.

FAIR pledges of a fruitful tree,
    Why do ye fall so fast?
    Your date is not so past,
But you may stay yet here awhile
    To blush and gently smile,
        And go at last.

What, were ye born to be,
    An hour or half's delight,
    And so to bid good-night?
'Twas pity Nature brought ye forth
    Merely to show your worth,
        And lose you quite.

But you are lovely leaves, where we
    May read how soon things have
    Their end, though ne'er so brave:
And after they have shown their pride,
    Like you, awhile, they glide
    Into the grave.

R. Herrick.

THE SUNFLOWER.

AH! Sunflower, weary of time,
    Who countest the steps of the sun;
Seeking after that sweet golden clime
    Where the traveller's journey is done;

Where the Youth pined away with desire,
    And the pale virgin shrouded in snow,
Arise from their graves, and aspire
    Where my Sunflower wishes to go!

W. Blake.

LOVE-SLAIN.

COME away, come away, Death,
And in sad cypress let me be laid;
    Fly away, fly away, breath;
I am slain by a fair cruel maid.
My shroud of white, stuck all with yew,
        O, prepare it!
My part of death no one so true
        Did share it.

    Not a flower, not a flower sweet,
On my black coffin let there be strown;
    Not a friend, not a friend greet
My poor corpse, where my bones shall be thrown.
A thousand thousand sighs to save,
        Lay me, O, where
Sad true lover ne'er find my grave,
        To weep there.

W. Shakespeare.

CONSTANCY.

LAY a garland on my hearse
  Of the dismal yew;
Maidens, willow branches bear;
  Say, I died true.

My love was false, but I was firm
  From my hour of birth.
Upon my buried body lie
  Lightly, gentle earth!

J. Fletcher.

INCONSTANCY.

TAKE, O take those lips away,
  That so sweetly were forsworn;
And those eyes, the break of day,
  Lights that do mislead the morn:
But my kisses bring again,
Seals of love, but seal'd in vain.

Hide, O hide those hills of snow,
  Which thy frozen bosom bears,
On whose tops the pinks that grow
  Are of those that April wears:
But first set my poor heart free,
Bound in those icy chains by thee.

W. Shakespeare.

LOVE UNRETURNED.

My silks and fine array,
  My smiles and languished air,
By love are driven away;
  And mournful lean Despair
Brings me yew to deck my grave:
Such end true lovers have.

His face is fair as heaven
  When springing buds unfold;
Oh, why to him was't given,
  Whose heart is wintry cold?
His breast is love's all-worshipp'd tomb,
Where all love's pilgrims come.

Bring me an axe and spade,
  Bring me a winding sheet;
When I my grave have made,
  Let winds and tempests beat:
Then down I'll lie, as cold as clay.
True love doth pass away!

W. Blake.

THE MAD MAIDEN'S SONG.

GOOD-MORROW to the day so fair,
  Good-morrow, sir, to you;
Good-morrow to mine own torn hair,
  Bedabbled all with dew.

Good-morrow to this primrose, too;
  Good-morrow to each maid
That will with flowers the tomb bestrew
  Wherein my love is laid.

Ah, woe is me—woe, woe is me,
  Alack and well-a-day!
For pity, sir, find out that bee
  Which bore my love away.

I'll seek him in your bonnet brave;
  I'll seek him in your eyes;
Nay, now I think they've made his grave
  In the bed of strawberries.

I'll seek him there! I know ere this
  The cold, cold earth doth shake him;
But I will go, or send a kiss
  By you, sir, to awake him.

Pray hurt him not; though he be dead,
  He knows well who do love him,
And who with green turfs rear his head,
  And who so rudely move him.

He's soft and tender, pray take heed;
  With bands of cowslips bind him,
And bring him home; but 'tis decreed
  That I shall never find him.

R. Herrick.

MAD SONG.

"THE wild winds weep,
   And the night is a-cold;
Come hither, sleep,
   And my griefs enfold! . . .
But lo! the morning peeps
Over the eastern steeps,
And the rustling beds of dawn
The earth do scorn.

Lo! to the vault
   Of pavèd heaven,
With sorrow fraught,
   My notes are driven:
They strike the ear of Night,
   Make weep the eyes of Day;
They make mad the roaring winds
   And with tempests play.

Like a fiend in a cloud,
   With howling woe
After night I do crowd,
   And with night do go;
I turn my back to the East
From whence comforts have increased;
For light doth seize my brain
With frantic pain."

W. Blake.

ARIEL'S SONG.

WHERE the bee sucks, there suck I;
  In a cowslip's bell I lie;
There I couch when owls do cry;
On the bat's back do I fly
  After sunset merrily:
Merrily, merrily shall I live now,
Under the blossom that hangs on the bough!

W. Shakespeare.

A FAIRY'S SONG.

OVER hill, over dale,
  Thorough bush, thorough brier,
Over park, over pale,
  Thorough flood, thorough fire,
I do wander everywhere,
Swifter than the moon's sphere;
And I serve the fairy queen,
To dew her orbs upon the green;
The cowslips tall her pensioners be;
In their gold coats spots you see;
These be rubies, fairy favours,
In those freckles live their savours:
I must go seek some dewdrops here,
And hang a pearl in every cowslip's ear.

W. Shakespeare.

THE FAIRY QUEEN.

COME follow, follow me,
  You, fairy elves that be:
  Which circle on the greene,
  Come follow Mab your queene.
Hand in hand let's dance around,
For this place is fairye ground.

  When mortals are at rest,
  And snoring in their nest;
  Unheard, and unespy'd,
  Through key-holes we do glide;
Over tables, stools, and shelves,
We trip it with our fairy elves.

  Upon a mushroome's head
  Our table-cloth we spread;
  A grain of rye, or wheat,
  Is manchet, which we eat;
Pearly drops of dew we drink,
In acorn cups fill'd to the brink.

  The brains of nightingales,
  With unctuous fat of snailes,
  Between two cockles stew'd,
  Is meat that's easily chew'd;
Tailes of wormes, and marrow of mice,
Do make a dish that's wondrous nice.

The grasshopper, gnat, and fly,
Serve for our minstrelsie;
Grace said, we dance a while,
And so the time beguile:
And if the moon doth hide her head,
The gloe-worm lights us home to bed.

On tops of dewie grasse
So nimbly do we passe,
The young and tender stalk
Ne'er bends when we do walk:
Yet in the morning may be seen
Where we the night before have been.

Anonymous.

SONG OF AN ENCHANTRESS.

LOVE is the blossom where there blows
Every thing that lives or grows;
Love doth make the heavens to move,
And the sun doth burn in love:
Love, the strong and weak doth yoke,
And makes the ivy climb the oak
Under whose shadows lions wild,
Soften'd by love, grow tame and mild.
Love, no med'cine can appease;
He burns the fishes in the seas;
Not all the skill his wounds can stanch.
Not all the sea his thirst can quench.
Love did make the bloody spear
Once a leafy coat to wear,
While in his leaves there shrouded lay
Sweet birds, for love that sing and play;
And of all love's joyful flame
I the bud and blossom am.
    Only lend thy knee to me,
    Thy wooing shall thy winning be!

See, see, the flowers that below
Now freshly as the morning blow,
And of all, the virgin rose,
That as bright Aurora shows;
How they all unleaved die,
Losing their virginity:

Like unto a summer shade,
But now born, and now they fade!
Every thing doth pass away;
There is danger in delay.
Come, come, gather then the rose;
Gather it, or it you lose.
All the sand of Tagus' shore
In my bosom casts its ore:
All the valleys' swimming corn
To my house is yearly borne:
Every grape of every vine
Is gladly bruised to make me wine;
While ten thousand kings, as proud
To carry up my train, have bow'd,
And a world of ladies send me
In my chamber to attend me:
All the stars in heaven that shine,
And ten thousand more, are mine.
    Only bend thy knee to me,
    Thy wooing shall thy winning be!

Giles Fletcher.

A VISION OF "THE FAERY QUEEN."

METHOUGHT I saw the grave where Laura lay,
Within that temple where the vestal flame
Was wont to burn; and, passing by that way,
To see that buried dust of living fame
Whose tomb fair Love and fairer Virtue kept,
All suddenly I saw the *Faery Queen*:
At whose approach the soul of Petrarke wept,
And from thenceforth those Graces were not seen
(For they this Queen attended); in whose stead
Oblivion laid him down on Laura's hearse.
Hereat the hardest stones were seen to bleed,
And groans of buried ghosts the heavens did perse;
  Where Homer's sprighte did tremble all for grief,
  And curst the access of that celestial thief.

Sir W. Raleigh.

HERSELF ALL TREASURE.

YE tradefull Merchants, that, with weary toyle
Do seeke most pretious things to make your gain;
And both the Indias of their treasure spoile;
What needeth you to seeke so farre in vaine?
For loe, my Love doth in herselfe containe
All this world's riches that may farre be found:
If Saphyres, loe, her eies be Saphyres plaine;
If Rubies, loe, hir lips be Rubies sound;
If Pearles, hir teeth be Pearles, both pure and round;
If Ivorie, her forhead Ivorie weene;
If Gold, her locks are finest Gold on ground:
If Silver, her faire hands are Silver sheene:
 But that which fairest is, but few behold—
 Her mind adornd with vertues manifold.

E. Spenser.

TO HIS LOVE.

WHEN in the chronicle of wasted time
I see descriptions of the fairest wights,
And beauty making beautiful old rhyme
In praise of ladies dead, and lovely knights;

Then in the blazon of sweet beauty's best
Of hand, of foot, of lip, of eye, of brow,
I see their antique pen would have exprest
Ev'n such a beauty as you master now.

So all their praises are but prophecies
Of this our time, all, you prefiguring;
And for they look'd but with divining eyes,
They had not skill enough your worth to sing:

For we, which now behold these present days,
Have eyes to wonder, but lack tongues to praise.

W. Shakespeare.

THE LOVER UNBELOVED LAMENTS BY NIGHT.

ALAS! so all things now do hold their peace!
Heaven and earth disturbèd in no thing;
The beasts, the air, the birds their song do cease;
The nightès car the stars about doth bring.
Calm is the sea; the waves work less and less:
So am not I, whom love, alas! doth wring,
Bringing before my face the great increase
Of my desires, whereat I weep and sing,
In joy and woe, as in a doubtful ease.
For my sweet thoughts sometime do pleasure bring;
But by and by, the cause of my disease
Gives me a pang, that inwardly doth sting
   When that I think what grief it is again
   To live, and lack the thing should rid my pain.

H. Howard (Earl of Surr

LOVE'S SHADOW.

FROM you have I been absent in the spring,
When proud-pied April, dress'd in all his trim,
Hath put a spirit of youth in everything;
That heavy Saturn laughed and leap'd with him.
Yet nor the lays of birds, nor the sweet smell
Of different flowers in odour and in hue,
Could make me any summer's story tell,
Or from their proud lap pluck them where they grew:
Nor did I wonder at the lilies white,
Nor praise the deep vermilion in the rose:
They were but sweet, but figures of delight,
Drawn after you, you, pattern of all those.
   Yet seem'd it winter still, and you away,
   As with your shadow I with these did play.

W. Shakespeare.

LOVE'S OMNIPRESENCE.

WERE I as base as is the lowly plain,
And you, my Love, as high as heaven above,
Yet should the thoughts of me your humble swain
Ascend to heaven, in honour of my Love.

Were I as high as heaven above the plain,
And you, my Love, as humble and as low
As are the deepest bottoms of the main,
Whereso'er you were, with you my love should go.

Were you the earth, dear Love, and I the skies,
My love should shine on you like to the sun,
And look upon you with ten thousand eyes
Till heaven wax'd blind, and till the world were done.

Whereso'er I am, below, or else above you,
Whereso'er you are, my heart shall truly love you.

Joshua Sylvestre.

TRUTH THE SOUL OF BEAUTY.

O HOW much more doth beauty beauteous seem
By that sweet ornament that truth doth give!
The rose looks fair, but fairer we it deem
For that sweet odour which doth in it live.
The canker-blooms have full as deep a dye
As the perfumèd tincture of the roses,
Hang on such thorns and play as wantonly
When summer's breath their maskèd buds discloses;
But, for their virtue only is their show,
They live unwooed, and unrespected fade;
Die to themselves.   Sweet roses do not so:
Of their sweet deaths are sweetest odours made.
  And so of you, beauteous and lovely youth,
  When that shall fade, my verse distills your truth.

W. Shakespeare.

THE PAINS OF MEMORY.

ALEXIS, here she stayed; among these pines,
Sweet hermitress, she did alone repair;
Here did she spread the treasure of her hair,
More rich than that brought from the Colchian mines;
She sat her by these muskèd eglantines,—
(The happy place the print seems yet to bear)—
Her voice did sweeten here thy sugar'd lines,
To which winds, trees, beasts, birds, did lend an ear;
Me here she first perceived, and here a morn
Of bright carnations did o'erspread her face;
Here did she sigh, here first my hopes were born,
And first I got a pledge of promised grace;
   But ah! what served it to be happy so,
   Sith passèd pleasures double but new woe?

W. Drummond.

ON HIS BLINDNESS.

WHEN I consider how my light is spent
Ere half my days, in this dark world and wide,
And that one talent which is death to hide
Lodged with me useless, though my soul more bent

To serve therewith my Maker, and present
My true account, lest he returning chide,—
Doth God exact day-labour, light denied?
I fondly ask:—But Patience, to prevent

That murmur, soon replies; God doth not need
Either man's work, or his own gifts: who best
Bear his mild yoke, they serve him best: His state

Is kingly: thousands at his bidding speed
And post o'er land and ocean without rest:—
They also serve who only stand and wait.

J. Milton.

TO MR. LAWRENCE.

LAWRENCE, of virtuous father virtuous son,
Now that the fields are dank and ways are mire,
Where shall we sometimes meet, and by the fire
Help waste a sullen day, what may be won

From the hard season gaining? Time will run
On smoother, till Favonius re-inspire
The frozen earth, and clothe in fresh attire
The lily and rose, that neither sow'd nor spun.

What neat repast shall feast us, light and choice,
Of Attic taste, with wine, whence we may rise
To hear the lute well touch'd, or artful voice

Warble immortal notes and Tuscan air?
He who of those delights can judge, and spare
To interpose them oft, is not unwise.

J. Milton.

IN PRAISE OF DAPHNE.

My Daphne's hair is twisted gold,
Bright stars a-piece her eyes do hold,
My Daphne's brow enthrones the graces,
My Daphne's beauty stains all faces,
On Daphne's cheek grow rose and cherry,
But Daphne's lip a sweeter berry;
Daphne's snowy hand but touched does melt,
And then no heavenlier warmth is felt;
My Daphne's voice tunes all the spheres,
My Daphne's music charms all ears;
Fond am I thus to sing her praise,
These glories now are turned to bays.

J. Lylye.

HER GOLDEN HAIR.

AMARANTHA, sweet and fair,
O braid no more that shining hair!
Let it fly, as unconfined
As its calm ravisher, the wind;
Who hath left his darling east
To wanton o'er that spicy nest.
Ev'ry tress must be confest,
But neatly tangled at the best—
Like a clew of golden thread
Most excellently ravelléd;
Do not, then, wind up that light
In ribbons, and o'ercloud in night,
Like the sun's in early ray;
But shake your head, and scatter day!

Colonel Lovelace.

A WARNING TO BEAUTY.

Sweet, be not proud of those two eyes
Which star-like sparkle in their skies;
Nor be you proud that you can see
All hearts your captives, yours yet free.
Be you not proud of that rich hair
Which wantons with the love-sick air;
Whenas that ruby which you wear
Sunk from the tip of your soft ear,
Will last to be a precious stone
When all your world of beauty's gone.

R. Herrick.

AGAINST WEEPING.

Dry those fair, those crystal eyes,
Which like growing fountains rise
To drown their banks; grief's sullen brooks
Would better flow in furrowed looks.
Thy lovely face was never meant
To be the shore of discontent.

Then clear those waterish stars again,
Which else portend a lasting rain;
Lest the clouds which settle there
Prolong my winter all the year,
And thy example others make
In love with sorrow for thy sake.

Dr. H. King.

A WELCOME.

Welcome, welcome! do I sing—
Far more welcome than the spring:
He that parteth from you never,
Shall enjoy a spring forever.

Love, that to the voice is near,
  Breaking from your ivory pale,
Need not walk abroad to hear
  The delightful nightingale.

Love, that looks still on your eyes,
  Though the winter have begun
To benumb our arteries,
  Shall not want the summer's sun.

Love, that still may see your cheeks,
  Where all rareness still reposes,
Is a fool if e'er he seeks
  Other lilies, other roses.

Love, to whom your soft lip yields,
  And perceives your breath in kissing,
All the odors of the fields
  Never, never shall be missing.

Love, that question would renew
  What fair Eden was of old,
Let him rightly study you,
  And a brief of that behold.

W. Browne.

TO CHLOE,

WHO WISHED HERSELF YOUNG
ENOUGH FOR ME.

CHLOE, why wish you that your years
　　Would backwards run till they met mine,—
That perfect likeness, which endears
　　Things unto things, might us combine?
Our ages so in date agree,
That twins do differ more than we.

There are two births: the one when light
　　First strikes the new awakened sense;
The other when two souls unite;
　　And we must count our life from thence:
When you loved me, and I loved you,
Then both of us were born anew.

Love then to us did new souls give,
　　And in those souls did plant new powers:
Since when another life we live,
　　The breath we breathe is his, not ours;
Love makes those young whom age doth chill,
And whom he finds young, keeps young still.

Love, like that angel that shall call
  Our bodies from the silent grave,
Unto one age doth raise us all;
  None too much, none too little have;
Nay, that the difference may be none,
He makes two not alike, but one.

And now, since you and I are such,
  Tell me what's yours, and what is mine?
Our eyes, our ears, our taste, smell, touch,
  Do, like our souls, in one combine:
So, by this, I as well may be
Too old for you, as you for me.

William Cartwright.

LOVE'S OMNIPOTENCE.

WHEN, dearest, I but think on thee,
Methinks all things that lovely be
  Are present, and my soul 's delighted;
For beauties that from worth arise
Are like the grace of deities,
  Still present with us, though unsighted.

Thus while I sit and sigh the day
With all his spreading lights away,
  Till night's black wings do overtake me,
Thinking on thee; thy beauties then,
As sudden lights do sleeping men,
  So they by their bright rays awake me.

Thus absence dies, and dying proves
No absence can consist with loves
  That do partake of fair perfection;
Since in the darkest night they may,
By their quick motion, find a way
  To see each other by reflection.

The waving sea can with such flood
Bathe some high palace that hath stood
  Far from the main up in the river;
Oh, think not then but love can do
As much, for that's an ocean too
  That flows not every day, but ever.

Owen Feltham.

TELL ME, MY HEART.

WHEN Delia on the plain appears,
Awed by a thousand tender fears,
I would approach, but dare not move;—
Tell me, my heart, if this be love?

Whene'er she speaks, my ravish'd ear
No other voice than her's can hear;
No other wit but her's approve;—
Tell me, my heart, if this be love?

If she some other swain commend,
Tho' I was once his fondest friend,
His instant enemy I prove;—
Tell me, my heart, if this be love?

When she is absent, I no more
Delight in all that pleased before,
The clearest spring, the shadiest grove;—
Tell me, my heart, if this be love?

When fond of power, of beauty vain,
Her nets she spread for every swain,
I strove to hate, but vainly strove;—
Tell me, my heart, if this be love?

Lord Lyttleton.

TO HIS DEAD LOVE.

TELL me, thou soul of her I love,
   Ah! tell me, whither art thou fled;
To what delightful world above,
   Appointed for the happy dead?

Or dost thou, free, at pleasure, roam,
   And sometimes share thy lover's woe;
Where, void of thee, his cheerless home
   Can now, alas! no comfort know?

Oh! if thou hover'st round my walk,
   While, under every well-known tree,
I to thy fancy'd shadow talk,
   And every tear is full of thee;

Should then the weary eye of grief,
   Beside some sympathetic stream,
In slumber find a short relief,
   Oh, visit thou my soothing dream!

James Thomson.

FRIENDS DEPARTED.

THEY are all gone into the world of light!
    And I alone sit ling'ring here!
Their very memory is fair and bright,
    And my sad thoughts doth clear.

It glows and glitters in my cloudy breast
    Like stars upon some gloomy grove,
Or those faint beams in which this hill is drest
    After the Sun's remove.

I see them walking in an air of glory,
    Whose light doth trample on my days;
My days, which are at best but dull and hoary,
    Mere glimmering and decays.

O holy Hope! and high Humility!
    High as the Heavens above!
These are your walks, and you have shew'd them me
    To kindle my cold love.

Dear, beauteous death; the Jewel of the Just!
    Shining no where but in the dark;
What mysteries do lie beyond thy dust,
    Could man outlook that mark!

He that hath found some fledg'd bird's nest may know
    At first sight if the bird be flown;
But what fair dell or grove he sings in now,
    That is to him unknown.

And yet, as Angels in some brighter dreams
    Call to the soul when man doth sleep,
So some strange thoughts transcend our wonted themes,
    And into glory peep.

If a star were confin'd into a tomb,
    Her captive flames must needs burn there;
But when the hand that lock'd her up gives room,
    She'll shine through all the sphere.

O Father of eternal life, and all
    Created glories under thee!
Resume thy spirit from this world of thrall
    Into true liberty!

Either disperse these mists which blot and fill
    My perspective still as they pass;
Or else remove me hence unto that hill
    Where I shall need no glass,

               H. Vaughan.

THE DYING MAN IN HIS GARDEN.

WHY, Damon, with the forward day
Dost thou thy little spot survey,
From tree to tree, with doubtful cheer,
Pursue the progress of the year,
What winds arise, what rains descend,
When thou before that year shalt end?

What do thy noontide walks avail,
To clear the leaf, and pick the snail,
Then wantonly to death decree
An insect usefuller than thee?
Thou and the worm are brother-kind,
As low, as earthy, and as blind.

Vain wretch! canst thou expect to see
The downy peach make court to thee?
Or that thy sense shall ever meet
The bean-flower's deep-embosom'd sweet
Exhaling with an evening blast?
Thy evenings then will all be past!

Thy narrow pride, thy fancied green
(For vanity's in little seen),
All must be left when Death appears,
In spite of wishes, groans, and tears;
Nor one of all thy plants that grow,
But Rosemary, will with thee go.

George Sewell.

THE WISDOM OF AGE.

THE seas are quiet when the winds give o'er
So calm are we when passions are no more.
For then we know how vain it was to boast
Of fleeting things, too certain to be lost.
Clouds of affection from our younger eyes
Conceal that emptiness which age descries.

The soul's dark cottage, batter'd and decay'd,
Lets in new light through chinks that time has made;
Stronger by weakness, wiser men become
As they draw near to their eternal home.
Leaving the old, both worlds at once they view,
That stand upon the threshold of the new.

E. Waller.

THE GIFT OF REST.

WHEN God at first made Man,
Having a glass of blessings standing by;
Let us (said he) pour on him all we can:
Let the world's riches, which dispersèd lie,
    Contract into a span.

So strength first made a way;
Then beauty flow'd; then wisdom, honour, pleasure:
When almost all was out, God made a stay,
Perceiving that alone, of all his treasure,
    Rest in the bottom lay.

For if I should (said he)
Bestow this jewel also on my creature,
He would adore my gifts instead of me,
And rest in Nature, not the God of Nature:
    So both should losers be.

Yet let him keep the rest,
But keep them with repining restlessness:
Let him be rich and weary, that at least,
If goodness lead him not, yet weariness
    May toss him to my breast.

G. Herbert.

MAN THE MICROCOSM.

MY God, I heard this day
That none doth build a stately habitation
   But he that means to dwell therein.
   What house more stately hath there been,
Or can be, than is Man, to whose creation
   All things are in decay?

   For Man is everything;
And more.   He is a tree, yet bears no fruit.
   A beast; yet is, or should be more.
   Reason and speech we only bring.
Parrots may thank us, if they are not mute;
   They go upon the score.

   Man is all symmetry,
Full of proportions, one limb to another,
   And to all the world besides.
   Each part may call the farthest brother;
For head with foot hath private amity,
   And both, with moons and tides.

   Nothing hath got so far
But Man hath caught and kept it as his prey.
   His eyes dismount the highest star;
   He is, in little, all the sphere.
Herbs gladly cure our flesh, because that they
   Find their acquaintance there.

For us the winds do blow,
The earth doth rest, heav'n move, and fountains flow.
　Nothing we see, but means our good,
　As our delight or as our treasure.
The whole is either our cupboard of food,
　　Or cabinet of pleasure.

　The stars have us to bed;
Night draws the curtain, which the sun withdraws.
　Music and light attend our head.
　All things unto our flesh are kind
In their descent and being; to our mind,
　　In their ascent and cause.

　Each thing is full of duty:
Waters united are our navigation;
　Distinguishèd, our habitation;
　Below, our drink; above, our meat;
Both are our cleanliness.　Hath one such beauty?
　　Then how are all things neat!

　More servants wait on Man
Than he'll take notice of.　In ev'ry path
　He treads down that which doth befriend him,
　When sickness makes him pale and wan.
Oh, mighty love! Man is one world, and hath
　　Another to attend him.

　Since, then, my God, thou hast
So brave a palace built, oh, dwell in it,
　That it may dwell with thee at last!
　Till then, afford us so much wit
That, as the world serves us, we may serve thee,
　　And both thy servants be.

　　　　　　　　　　　　　　G. Herbert.

THE HERMIT.

AT the close of the day, when the hamlet is still,
  And mortals the sweets of forgetfulness prove;
When nought but the torrent is heard on the hill,
  And nought but the nightingale's song in the grove;
'Twas thus, by the cave of the mountain afar,
  While his harp rang symphonious, a hermit began;
No more with himself, or with nature, at war,
  He thought as a sage, though he felt as a man.

"Ah! why thus abandon'd to darkness and woe?
  Why lone Philomela, that languishing fall?
For spring shall return, and a lover bestow,
  And sorrow no longer thy bosom enthral.
But, if pity inspire thee, renew the sad lay;
  Mourn, sweetest complainer; man calls thee to mourn.
O, soothe him, whose pleasures like thine pass away:
  Full quickly they pass—but they never return.

"Now gliding remote, on the verge of the sky,
  The moon half extinguish'd her crescent displays;
But lately I mark'd, when majestic on high
  She shone, and the planets were lost in her blaze.
Roll on, thou fair orb, and with gladness pursue
  The path that conducts thee to splendour again:
But man's faded glory what change shall renew?
  Ah, fool! to exult in a glory so vain!

" 'Tis night, and the landscape is lovely no more:
   I mourn; but ye woodlands, I mourn not for you;
For morn is approaching, your charms to restore,
   Perfumed with fresh fragrance and glittering with dew:
Nor yet for the ravage of winter I mourn;
   Kind nature the embryo blossom will save;
But when shall spring visit the mouldering urn?
   O, when shall day dawn on the night of the grave?

" 'Twas thus, by the light of false science betray'd,
   That leads to bewilder, and dazzles to blind,
My thoughts wont to roam, from shade onward to shade,
   Destruction before me, and sorrow behind.
"O, pity, great Father of light,' then I cried,
   'Thy creature, that fain would not wander from Thee:
Lo, humbled in dust, I relinquish my pride:
   From doubt and from darkness Thou only canst free!'

"And darkness and doubt are now flying away;
   No longer I roam in conjecture forlorn:
So breaks on the traveller, faint and astray,
   The bright and the balmy effulgence of morn.
See Truth, Love, and Mercy, in triumph descending,
   And Nature all glowing in Eden's first bloom!
On the cold cheek of Death smiles and roses are blending,
   And Beauty immortal awakes from the tomb!"

James Beattie.

ALEXANDER SELKIRK.

I AM monarch of all I survey;
My right there is none to dispute;
From the centre all round to the sea
I am lord of the fowl and the brute.
O Solitude! where are the charms
That sages have seen in thy face?
Better dwell in the midst of alarms
Than reign in this horrible place.

I am out of humanity's reach,
I must finish my journey alone,
Never hear the sweet music of speech;
I start at the sound of my own.
The beasts that roam over the plain
My form with indifference see;
They are so unacquainted with man,
Their tameness is shocking to me.

Society, Friendship, and Love
Divinely bestow'd upon man,
O had I the wings of a dove
How soon would I taste you again!
My sorrows I then might assuage
In the ways of religion and truth,
Might learn from the wisdom of age,
And be cheer'd by the sallies of youth.

Ye winds that have made me your sport,
Convey to this desolate shore
Some cordial endearing report
Of a land I shall visit no more:
My friends, do they now and then send
A wish or a thought after me?
O tell me I yet have a friend,
Though a friend I am never to see.

How fleet is a glance of the mind!
Compared with the speed of its flight,
The tempest itself lags behind,
And the swift-wingéd arrows of light.
When I think of my own native land
In a moment I seem to be there;
But alas! recollection at hand
Soon hurries me back to despair.

But the seafowl is gone to her nest,
The beast is laid down in his lair;
Even here is a season of rest,
And I to my cabin repair.
There's mercy in every place,
And mercy, encouraging thought!
Gives even affliction a grace
And reconciles man to his lot.

William Cowper.

ODE TO LEVEN WATER.

On Leven's banks, while free to rove,
And tune the rural pipe to love,
I envied not the happiest swain
That ever trod the Arcadian plain.
      Pure stream, in whose transparent wave
My youthful limbs I wont to lave;
No torrents stain thy limpid source,
No rocks impede thy dimpling course,
That sweetly warbles o'er its bed,
With white, round, polish'd pebbles spread;
While, lightly poised, the scaly brood
In myriads cleave thy crystal flood;
The springing trout in speckled pride;
The salmon, monarch of the tide;
The ruthless pike, intent on war;
The silver eel and mottled par.
Devolving from thy parent lake,
A charming maze thy waters make,
By bowers of birch and groves of pine,
And edges flowered with eglantine.
      Still on thy banks so gaily green
May numerous herds and flocks be seen;
And lasses chanting o'er the pail;
And shepherds piping in the dale;
And ancient faith that knows no guile;
And industry embrowned with toil;
And hearts resolved, and hands prepared,
The blessings they enjoy to guard!

Tobias Smollett.

A RURAL PICTURE.

SWEET Auburn! loveliest village of the plain,
Where health and plenty cheer'd the labouring swain;
Where smiling spring its earliest visit paid,
And parting summer's ling'ring blooms delay'd;
Dear lovely bowers of innocence and ease,
Seats of my youth, when every sport could please;
How often have I loiter'd o'er thy green,
Where humble happiness endear'd each scene!
How often have I paus'd on every charm,
The shelter'd cot, the cultivated farm,
The never-failing brook, the busy mill,
The decent church that topt the neighbouring hill,
The hawthorn bush, with seats beneath the shade,
For talking age and whispering lovers made!
          *   *   *   *
Sweet was the sound, when oft, at evening's close,
Up yonder hill the village murmur rose;
There, as I past with careless steps and slow,
The mingling notes came soften'd from below;
The swain responsive as the milk-maid sung;
The sober herd that low'd to meet their young;
The noisy geese that gabbled o'er the pool;
The playful children just let loose from school;
The watch-dog's voice, that bay'd the whispering wind,
And the loud laugh that spoke the vacant mind;
These all in sweet confusion sought the shade,
And fill'd each pause the nightingale had made.
          *   *   *   *
How blest is he who crowns, in shades like these,
A youth of labour with an age of ease;

Who quits a world where strong temptations try,
And, since 'tis hard to combat, learns to fly!
For him no wretches, born to work and weep,
Explore the mine, or tempt the dangerous deep;
Nor surly porter stands in guilty state,
To spurn imploring famine from the gate;
But on he moves to meet his latter end,
Angels around befriending virtue's friend;
Sinks to the grave with unperceiv'd decay,
While resignation gently slopes the way;
And, all his prospects brightening to the last,
His heaven commences ere the world be past.

Oliver Goldsmith.

MORNING.

WHAT tongue the melodies of morn can tell?
The wild-brook babbling down the mountain side;
The lowing herd; the sheepfold's simple bell;
The pipe of early shepherd dim descried
In the lone valley; echoing far and wide
The clamorous horn along the cliffs above;
The hollow murmur of the ocean-tide;
The hum of bees, and linnet's lay of love,
And the full choir that wakes the universal grove.

The cottage-curs at early pilgrim bark;
Crown'dwith her pail, the tripping milkmaid sings;
The whistling ploughman stalks afield; and, hark!
Down the rough slope the ponderous wagon rings;
Thro' rustling corn the hare astonish'd springs;
Slow tolls the village-clock the drowsy hour;
The partridge bursts away on whirring wings;
Deep mourns the turtle in sequester'd bower,
And shrill lark carols clear from her aërial tower.

J. Beattie.

EVENING.

IF aught of oaten stop or pastoral song
May hope, chaste Eve, to soothe thy modest ear
    Like thy own solemn springs,
    Thy springs, and dying gales;

O Nymph reserved,—while now the bright-hair'd sun
Sits in yon western tent, whose cloudy skirts
    With brede ethereal wove,
    O'erhang his wavy bed,

Now air is hush'd, save where the weak-eyed bat
With short shrill shriek flits by on leathern wing,
    Or where the beetle winds
    His small but sullen horn,

As oft he rises midst the twilight path,
Against the pilgrim borne in heedless hum,—
    Now teach me, maid composed,
    To breathe some soften'd strain

Whose numbers, stealing through thy dark'ning vale,
May not unseemly with its stillness suit;
    As musing slow I hail
    Thy genial loved return.

For when thy folding-star arising shows
His paly circlet, at his warning lamp
    The fragrant Hours, and Elves
    Who slept in buds the day,

And many a Nymph who wreathes her brows with sedge
And sheds the freshening dew, and lovelier still
    The pensive Pleasures sweet,
    Prepare thy shadowy car.

Then let me rove some wild and heathy scene;
Or find some ruin midst its dreary dells,
    Whose walls more awful nod
    By thy religious gleams.

Or if chill blustering winds or driving rain
Prevent my willing feet, be mine the hut
    That, from the mountain's side,
    Views wilds and swelling floods,

And hamlets brown, and dim-discover'd spires;
And hears their simple bell; and marks o'er all
    Thy dewy fingers draw
    The gradual dusky veil.

While Spring shall pour his showers, as oft he wont,
And bathe thy breathing tresses, meekest Eve!
    While Summer loves to sport
    Beneath thy lingering light;

While sallow Autumn fills thy lap with leaves;
Or Winter, yelling through the troublous air,
    Affrights thy shrinking train
    And rudely rends thy robes;

So long, regardful of thy quiet rule,
Shall Fancy, Friendship, Science, smiling Peace,
    Thy gentlest influence own,
    And love thy favourite name!

William Collins.

ELEGY,
WRITTEN IN A COUNTRY CHURCHYARD.

THE curfew tolls the knell of parting day,
The lowing herd winds slowly o'er the lea,
The ploughman homeward plods his weary way,
And leaves the world to darkness and to me.

Now fades the glimm'ring landscape on the sight,
And all the air a solemn stillness holds,
Save where the beetle wheels his droning flight,
 And drowsy tinklings lull the distant folds;

Save that from yonder ivy-mantled tower
The moping owl does to the moon complain
Of such as, wandering near her secret bower,
Molest her ancient solitary reign.

Beneath those rugged elms, that yew-tree's shade
Where heaves the turf in many a mouldering heap,
Each in his narrow cell for ever laid,
The rude Forefathers of the hamlet sleep.

The breezy call of incense-breathing morn,
The swallow twittering from the straw-built shed,
The cock's shrill clarion, or the echoing horn,
No more shall rouse them from their lowly bed.

For them no more the blazing hearth shall burn
Or busy housewife ply her evening care:
No children run to lisp their sire's return,
Or climb his knees the envied kiss to share.

Oft did the harvest to their sickle yield,
Their furrow oft the stubborn glebe has broke;
How jocund did they drive their team afield!
How bow'd the woods beneath their sturdy stroke!

Let not Ambition mock their useful toil,
Their homely joys, and destiny obscure;
Nor Grandeur hear with a disdainful smile
The short and simple annals of the Poor.

The boast of heraldry, the pomp of power,
And all that beauty, all that wealth e'er gave
Await alike th' inevitable hour:—
The paths of glory lead but to the grave.

Nor you, ye Proud, impute to these the fault
If Memory o'er their tomb no trophies raise,
Where through the long-drawn aisle and fretted vault
The pealing anthem swells the note of praise.

Can storied urn or animated bust
Back to its mansion call the fleeting breath?
Can Honour's voice provoke the silent dust,
Or Flattery soothe the dull cold ear of Death?

Perhaps in this neglected spot is laid
Some heart once pregnant with celestial fire;
Hands, that the rod of empire might have sway'd,
Or waked to ecstasy the living lyre:

But Knowledge to their eyes her ample page,
Rich with the spoils of time, did ne'er unroll;
Chill Penury repress'd their noble rage,
And froze the genial current of the soul.

Full many a gem of purest ray serene
The dark unfathom'd caves of ocean bear:
Full many a flower is born to blush unseen,
And waste its sweetness on the desert air.

Some village-Hampden, that with dauntless breast
The little tyrant of his fields withstood,
Some mute inglorious Milton here may rest,
Some Cromwell, guiltless of his country's blood.

Th' applause of list'ning senates to command,
The threats of pain and ruin to despise,
To scatter plenty o'er a smiling land,
And read their history in a nation's eyes

Their lot forbade: nor circumscribed alone
Their growing virtues, but their crimes confined;
Forbade to wade through slaughter to a throne,
And shut the gates of mercy on mankind;

The struggling pangs of conscious truth to hide,
To quench the blushes of ingenuous shame,
Or heap the shrine of Luxury and Pride
With incense kindled at the Muse's flame.

Far from the madding crowd's ignoble strife
Their sober wishes never learn'd to stray;
Along the cool sequester'd vale of life
They kept the noiseless tenour of their way.

Yet e'en these bones from insult to protect
Some frail memorial still erected nigh,
With uncouth rhymes and shapeless sculpture deck'd,
Implores the passing tribute of a sigh.

Their name, their years, spelt by th' unletter'd Muse,
The place of fame and elegy supply:
And many a holy text around she strews
That teach the rustic moralist to die.

For who, to dumb forgetfulness a prey,
This pleasing anxious being e'er resign'd,
Left the warm precincts of the cheerful day,
Nor cast one longing lingering look behind?

On some fond breast the parting soul relies,
Some pious drops the closing eye requires;
E'en from the tomb the voice of Nature cries,
E'en in our ashes live their wonted fires.

For thee, who, mindful of th' unhonour'd dead,
Dost in these lines their artless tale relate;
If chance, by lonely Contemplation led,
Some kindred spirit shall inquire thy fate,—

Haply some hoary-headed swain may say,
Oft have we seen him at the peep of dawn
Brushing with hasty steps the dews away,
To meet the sun upon the upland lawn;

There at the foot of yonder nodding beech
That wreathes its old fantastic roots so high,
His listless length at noon-tide would he stretch,
And pore upon the brook that babbles by.

Hard by yon wood, now smiling as in scorn,
Muttering his wayward fancies he would rove;
Now drooping, woeful-wan, like one forlorn,
Or crazed with care, or cross'd in hopeless love.

One morn I miss'd him on the custom'd hill,
Along the heath, and near his favourite tree;
Another came; nor yet beside the rill,
Nor up the lawn, nor at the wood was he;

The next with dirges due in sad array
Slow through the church-way path we saw him borne,—
Approach and read (for thou canst read) the lay
Graved on the stone beneath yon aged thorn.

THE EPITAPH.

Here rests his head upon the lap of Earth
A Youth, to Fortune and to Fame unknown;
Fair Science frown'd not on his humble birth,
And Melancholy mark'd him for her own.

Large was his bounty, and his soul sincere;
Heaven did a recompense as largely send:
He gave to Misery all he had, a tear;
He gain'd from Heaven, 'twas all he wish'd, a friend.

No farther seek his merits to disclose,
Or draw his frailties from their dread abode,
(There they alike in trembling hope repose,)
The bosom of his Father and his God.

Thomas Gray.

THE POPLAR FIELD.

THE poplars are fell'd, farewell to the shade
And the whispering sound of the cool colonnade;
The winds play no longer and sing in the leaves,
Nor Ouse on his bosom their image receives.

Twelve years have elapsed since I last took a view
Of my favourite field, and the bank where they grew:
And now in the grass behold they are laid,
And the tree is my seat that once lent me a shade.

The blackbird has fled to another retreat
Where the hazels afford him a screen from the heat;
And the scene where his melody charm'd me before
Resounds with his sweet-flowing ditty no more.

My fugitive years are all hasting away,
And I must ere long lie as lowly as they,
With a turf on my breast and a stone at my head,
Ere another such grove shall arise in its stead.

'Tis a sight to engage me, if anything can,
To muse on the perishing pleasures of man;
Short-lived as we are, our enjoyments, I see,
Have a still shorter date, and die sooner than we.

W. Cowper.

THE BIRKS OF INVERMAY.

THE smiling morn, the breathing spring,
Invite the tuneful birds to sing;
And, while they warble from the spray,
Love melts the universal lay.
Let us, Amanda, timely wise,
Like them improve the hour that flies;
And in soft raptures waste the day
Among the birks of Invermay.

For soon the winter of the year,
And age, life's winter, will appear:
At this thy living bloom will fade,
As that will strip the verdant shade.
Our taste of pleasure then is o'er—
The feathered songsters are no more;
And when they drop and we decay,
Adieu the birks of Invermay!

David Mallet.

TO THE CUCKOO.

TO THE CUCKOO.

HAIL, beauteous stranger of the grove!
  Thou messenger of Spring!
Now Heaven repairs thy rural seat,
  And woods thy welcome sing.

What time the daisy decks the green,
  Thy certain voice we hear;
Hast thou a star to guide thy path,
  Or mark the rolling year?

Delightful visitant! with thee
  I hail the time of flowers,
And hear the sound of music sweet
  From birds among the bowers.

The school-boy, wandering through the wood
  To pull the primrose gay,
Starts, the new voice of Spring to hear,
  And imitates thy lay.

What time the pea puts on the bloom
  Thou fliest thy vocal vale,
An annual guest in other lands,
  Another Spring to hail.

Sweet bird! thy bower is ever green,
   Thy sky is ever clear;
Thou hast no sorrow in thy song,
   No Winter in thy year!

O could I fly, I'd fly with thee!
   We'd make, with joyful wing,
Our annual visit o'er the globe,
   Companions of the Spring.

John Logan.

THE BIRD.

HITHER thou com'st.   The busie wind all night
Blew through thy lodging, where thy own warm wing
Thy pillow was.   Many a sullen storm,
For which coarse man seems much the fitter born,
     Rain'd on thy bed
     And harmless head;

And now as fresh and cheerful as the light
Thy little heart in early hymns doth sing
Unto that *Providence,* whose unseen arm
Curb'd them, and cloth'd thee well and warm.
    All things that be praise Him; and had
    Their lesson taught them when first made.

So hills and valleys into singing break;
And though poor stones have neither speech nor tongue,
While active winds and streams both run and speak,
Yet stones are deep in admiration.
Thus Praise and Prayer here beneath the sun
Make lesser mornings, when the great are done.

For each inclosed spirit is a star
    Inlightning his own little sphere,
Whose light, though fetcht and borrowed from far,
    Both mornings makes and evenings there.

But as these Birds of light make a land glad,
    Chirping their solemn matins on each tree:
    So in the shades of night some dark fowls be,
Whose heavy notes make all that hear them sad.

The turtle then in palm-trees mourns,
    While owls and satyrs howl;
The pleasant land to brimstone turns,
    And all her streams grow foul.

Brightness and mirth, and love and faith, all flye,
Till the day-spring breaks forth again from high.

                    H. Vaughan.

THE TIGER.

TIGER! Tiger! burning bright
In the forests of the night,
What immortal hand or eye
Fram'd thy fearful symmetry?

In what distant deeps or skies
Burn'd the fervour of thine eyes?
On what wings dar'd he aspire—
What the hand dar'd seize the fire?

And what shoulder and what art
Could twist the sinews of thy heart?
When thy heart began to beat,
What dread hand form'd thy dread feet?

What the hammer, what the chain
Formed thy strength and forged thy brain?
What the anvil? What dread grasp
Dar'd thy deadly terrors clasp?

When the stars threw down their spears,
And sprinkled heav'n with shining tears,
Did He smile, his work to see?
Did He who made the lamb make thee?

W. Blake.

THE FLY.

Busy, curious, thirsty fly,
Drink with me, and drink as I;
Freely welcome to my cup,
Couldst thou sip, and sip it up.
Make the most of life you may;
Life is short, and wears away.

Both alike are mine and thine,
Hastening quick to their decline;
Thine's a summer, mine's no more,
Though repeated to threescore;
Threescore summers, when they're gone,
Will appear as short as one.

Anonymous.

THE BIRDS' MESSAGE.

Ye little birds that sit and sing
　　Amidst the shady valleys,
And see how Phillis sweetly walks
　　Within her garden-alleys;
Go, pretty birds, about her bower;
Sing, pretty birds, she may not lower;
Ah, me! methinks I see her frown!
　　Ye pretty wantons, warble.

Go, tell her, through your chirping bills,
　As you by me are bidden,
To her is only known my love,
　Which from the world is hidden.
Go, pretty birds, and tell her so;
See that your notes strain not too low;
For still, methinks, I see her frown!
　Ye pretty wantons, warble.

Go, tune your voices' harmony,
　And sing, I am her lover;
Strain loud and sweet, that every note
　With sweet content may move her.
And she that hath the sweetest voice,
Tell her I will not change my choice;
Yet still, methinks, I see her frown!
　Ye pretty wantons, warble.

Oh, fly! make haste! see, see, she falls
　Into a pretty slumber.
Sing round about her rosy bed,
　That waking, she may wonder.
Say to her, 'tis her lover true
That sendeth love to you, to you;
And when you hear her kind reply,
　Return with pleasant warblings.

T. Heywood.

EXCHANGE NO ROBBERY.

I PRITHEE send me back my heart,
　　Since I cannot have thine;
For if from yours you will not part,
　　Why, then, shouldst thou have mine?

Yet now I think on't, let it lie,
　　To find it were in vain;
For thou'st a thief in either eye
　　Would steal it back again.

Why should two hearts in one breast lie,
　　And yet not lodge together?
O Love! where is thy sympathy,
　　If thus our breasts thou sever?

But love is such a mystery,
　　I cannot find it out;
For when I think I'm best resolv'd,
　　Then I am most in doubt.

Then farewell care, and farewell woe;
　　I will no longer pine;
For I'll believe I have her heart,
　　As much as she has mine.

Sir J. Suckling.

PHILLIS.

PHILLIS is my only joy,
  Faithless as the winds or seas;
Sometimes coming, sometimes coy,
  Yet she never fails to please.
        If with a frown
        I am cast down,
        Phillis smiling
        And beguiling,
Makes me happier than before.

Though, alas! too late I find
  Nothing can her fancy fix,
Yet the moment she is kind,
  I forgive her all her tricks;
        Which though I see,
        I can't get free;
        She deceiving,
        I believing,
What need lovers wish for more?

Sir C. Sedley.

UNGRATEFUL NANNY.

Did ever swain a nymph adore
  As I ungrateful Nanny do?
Was ever shepherd's heart so sore—
  Was ever broken heart so true?
My eyes are swelled with tears; but she
Has never shed a tear for me.

If Nanny called did Robin stay,
  Or linger when she bade me run?
She only had the word to say,
  And all she asked was quickly done:
I always thought on her; but she
Would ne'er bestow a thought on me.

To let her cows my clover taste,
  Have I not rose by break of day?
When did her heifers ever fast,
  If Robin in his yard had hay?
Though to my fields they welcome were,
I never welcome was to her!

If Nanny ever lost a sheep,
  I cheerfully did give her two:
Did not her lambs in safety sleep
  Within my folds in frost and snow?
Have they not there from cold been free?
But Nanny still is cold to me.

Whene'er I climb'd our orchard trees,
  The ripest fruit was kept for Nan;
Oh, how those hands that drown'd her bees
  Were stung, I'll ne'er forget the pain!
Sweet were the combs, as sweet could be;
But Nanny ne'er look'd sweet on me.

If Nanny to the well did come,
  'Twas I that did her pitchers fill;
Full as they were, I brought them home;
  Her corn I carried to the mill;
My back did bear her sacks; but she
Would never bear the sight of me.

To Nanny's poultry oats I gave,
  I'm sure they always had the best;
Within this week her pigeons have
  Eat up a peck of peas at least;
Her little pigeons kiss; but she
Would never take a kiss from me.

Must Robin always Nanny woo,
  And Nanny still on Robin frown?
Alas, poor wretch! what shall I do,
  If Nanny does not love me soon?
If no relief to me she'll bring,
I'll hang me in her apron string.

Charles Hamilton (Lord Binney).

THE PLAGUE OF LOVE.

O, WHAT a plague is love!
  I cannot bear it;
She will unconstant prove,
  I greatly fear it:
It so torments my mind
  That my heart faileth;
She wavers with the wind
  As a ship saileth.
Please her the best I may,
She loves still to gainsay:
Alack, and well-a day!
    Phillida flouts me.

At the fair, t'other day,
  As she passed by me,
She looked another way,
  And would not spy me.
I wooed her for to dine,
  But could not get her;
Dick had her to The Vine—
  He might intreat her;
With Daniel she did dance,
On me she would not glance:
O, thrice unhappy chance!
    Phillida flouts me.

Fair maid, be not so coy—
  Do not disdain me;
I am my mother's joy,—
  Sweet, entertain me!
I shall have, when she dies,
  All things that's fitting,—
Her poultry and her bees,
  And her goose sitting;
A pair of mattress beds,
A barrelful of shreds;
And yet, for all these gauds,
    Phillida flouts me!

I often heard her say
  That she loved posies:
In the last month of May
  I gave her roses;
Cowslips and gillyflowers,
  And the sweet lily,
I got to deck the bowers
  Of my dear Philly:
She did them all disdain,
And threw them back again:
Therefore 'tis flat and plain,
    Phillida flouts me.

Thou shalt eat curds and cream
  All the year lasting,
And drink the crystal stream,
  Pleasant in tasting;
Swig whey until thou burst,
  Eat bramble-berries,
Pye-lid and pastry crust,
  Pears, plums, and cherries;
Thy garments shall be thin,
Made of a wether's skin:
Yet, all's not worth a pin,—
    Phillida flouts me!

Which way soe'er I go,
  She still torments me;
And whatsoe'er I do,
  Nothing contents me.
I fade and pine away,
  With grief and sorrow;
I fall quite to decay,
  Like any shadow:
I shall be dead, I **fear**,
Within a thousand year;
And all because my dear
    Phillida flouts me.

Fair maiden, have a care!
  And in time take me;
I can have those as fair,
  If you forsake me:
There's Doll, the dairy-maid,
  Smiled on me lately;
And Wanton Winifred
  Favors me greatly:
She throws milk on my clothes,
Th' other plays with my nose:
What pretty toys are those!
    Phillida flouts me.

She has a cloth of mine,
  Wrought with blue coventry,
Which she keeps as a sign
  Of my fidelity;
But if she frowns on me,
  She ne'er shall wear it:
I'll give it my maid Joan,
  And she shall tear it.
Since 'twill no better be,
I'll bear it patiently;
Yet all the world may see
    Phillida flouts me.

Anonymous.

ON THE DEATH OF A FAVOURITE CAT,

DROWNED IN A TUB OF GOLD FISHES.

'TWAS on a lofty vase's side,
Where China's gayest art had dyed
  The azure flowers, that blow;
Demurest of the tabby kind,
The pensive Selima, reclined,
  Gazed on the lake below.

Her conscious tail her joy declared;
The fair round face, the snowy beard,
  The velvet of her paws,
Her coat, that with the tortoise vies,
Her ears of jet, and emerald eyes,
  She saw; and purr'd applause.

Still had she gazed; but midst the tide
Two angel forms were seen to glide,
  The Genii of the stream:
Their scaly armour's Tyrian hue
Through richest purple to the view
  Betray'd a golden gleam.

The hapless Nymph with wonder saw:
A whisker first, and then a claw,
  With many an ardent wish,
She stretch'd in vain, to reach the prize:
What female heart can gold despise?
  What Cat's averse to fish?

Presumptuous Maid! with looks intent
Again she stretch'd, again she bent,
　　Nor knew the gulf between:
(Malignant Fate sat by, and smiled:)
The slippery verge her feet beguiled,
　　She tumbled headlong in.

Eight times emerging from the flood
She mew'd to every watery God
　　Some speedy aid to send:—
No Dolphin came, no Nereid stirr'd,
Nor cruel Tom nor Susan heard—
　　A favourite has no friend!

From hence, ye Beauties! undeceived
Know one false step is ne'er retrieved,
　　And be with caution bold:
Not all that tempts your wandering eyes
And heedless hearts, is lawful prize,
　　Nor all that glisters, gold!

T. Gray.

CUPID'S MISTAKE.

As after noon, one summer's day
  Venus stood bathing in a river,
Cupid a-shooting went that way,
  New strung his bow, new fill'd his quiver.

With skill he chose his sharpest dart;
  With all his might his bow he drew;
Swift to his beauteous parent's heart
  The too-well guided arrow flew.

"I faint! I die!" the goddess cried:
  "Oh, cruel! couldst thou find no other
To wreak thy spleen on, Parricide?
  Like Nero, thou hast slain thy mother!

Poor Cupid, sobbing, scarce could speak;
  "Indeed, Mamma, I did not know ye.
Alas! how easy my mistake!
  I took you for your likeness—Chloe."

Matthew Prior.

HOW TO MAKE A BEAUTY.

(LINES TO MRS. BIDDY FLOYD.)

WHEN Cupid did his grandsire Jove entreat
To form some Beauty by a new receipt,
Jove sent and found, far in a country scene,
Truth, innocence, good-nature, look serene;
From which ingredients first the dexterous boy
Picked the demure, the awkward, and the coy.
The Graces from the court did next provide
Breeding and wit, and air, and decent pride:
These Venus clears from every spurious grain
Of nice, coquette, affected, pert, and vain.
   Jove mix'd up all, and his best clay employ'd;
   Then called the happy composition—FLOYD.

Jonathan Swift.

LOVE'S PATIENCE.

WHEN raging love with extreme pain
   Most cruelly distrains my heart;
When that my tears, as floods of rain,
   Bear witness of my woful smart;
When sighs have wasted so my breath,
That I lie at the point of death:

I call to mind the navy great
  That the Greeks brought to Troy town:
And how the boisterous winds did beat
  Their ships, and rent their sails adown;
Till Agamemnon's daughter's blood
Appeas'd the gods that them withstood;

And how that in those ten years war
  Full many bloody deed was done;
And many a lord that came full far,
  There caught his bane, alas! too soon;
And many a good knight overrun,
Before the Greeks had Helen won.

Then think I thus: "Sith such repair,
  So long time war of valiant men,
Was all to win a lady fair,
  Shall I not learn to suffer, then?
And think my life well spent to be
Serving a worthier wight than she?

Therefore I never will repent,
  But pains contented still endure;
For like as when, rough winter spent,
  The pleasing spring straight draweth in ure;
So after raging storms of care,
Joyful at length may be my fare.

H. Howard (Earl of Surrey)

LOVE'S MIGHT.

HEAR, ye ladies that despise,
  What the mighty love has done;
Fear examples, and be wise:
  Fair Calisto was a nun;
Leda, sailing on the stream
  To deceive the hopes of man,
Love accounting but a dream,
  Doated on a silver swan;
    Danaë, in a brazen tower
    Where no love was, loved a shower.

Hear, ye ladies that are coy,
  What the mighty love can do;
Fear the fierceness of the boy:
  The chaste moon he makes to woo;
Vesta, kindling holy fires,
  Circled round about with spies,
Never dreaming loose desires,
  Doting at the altar dies;
    Ilion, in a short hour, higher
    He can build, and once more fire.

Beaumont and Fletcher.

THE HEART OF STONE.

WHENCE comes my love? O heart, disclose;
It was from cheeks that shamed the rose,
From lips that spoil the ruby's praise,
From eyes that mock the diamond's blaze:
Whence comes my wo? As freely own;
Ah me! 'twas from a heart like stone.

The blushing cheek speaks modest mind,
The lips befitting words most kind,
The eye does tempt to love's desire,
And seems to say 'tis Cupid's fire;
Yet all so fair but speak my moan,
Sith nought doth say the heart of stone.

Why thus, my love, so kind bespeak
Sweet eye, sweet lip, sweet blushing cheek—
Yet not a heart to save my pain!
Oh Venus, take thy gifts again!
Make not so fair to cause our moan,
Or make a heart that's like our own.

Sir John Harrington.

CRUEL AND FAIR.

WHEN, cruel fair one, I am slain
    By thy disdain,
And, as a trophy of thy scorn,
  To some old tomb am borne,
Thy fetters must their power bequeath
    To those of Death;
  Nor can thy flame immortal burn,
Like monumental fires within an urn:
Thus freed from thy proud empire, I shall prove
There is more liberty in Death than Love.

And when forsaken lovers come
    To see my tomb,
Take heed thou mix not with the crowd,
  And, as a victor—proud
To view the spoils thy beauty made—
    Press near my shade,
  Lest thy too cruel breath or name
Should fan my ashes back into a flame,
And thou, devoured by this revengeful fire,
His sacrifice, who died as thine, expire.

But if cold earth or marble must
    Conceal my dust,
Whilst, hid in some dark ruins, I
  Dumb and forgotten lie,
The pride of all thy victory
    Will sleep with me;

And they who should attest thy glory
Will or forget or not believe this story.
Then, to increase the triumph, let me rest—
Since by thine eye slain, buried in thy breast.

Thomas Stanley.

LOVE'S PRISONER.

How sweet I roamed from field to field
  And tasted all the summer's pride,
Till I the Prince of Love beheld
  Who in the sunny beams did glide.

He show'd me lilies for my hair,
  And blushing roses for my brow;
He led me through his gardens fair
  Where all his golden pleasures grow.

With sweet May-dews my wings were wet,
  And Phœbus fired my vocal rage;
He caught me in his silken net,
  And shut me in his golden cage.

He loves to sit and hear me sing,
  Then, laughing, sports and plays with me;
Then stretches out my golden wing,
  And mocks my loss of liberty.

W. Blake.

TO NANCY.

O NANCY wilt thou go with me,
  Nor sigh to leave the flaunting town?
Can silent glens have charms for thee,
  The lowly cot and russet gown?
No longer drest in silken sheen,
  No longer deck'd with jewels rare,
Say, canst thou quit each courtly scene,
  Where thou wert fairest of the fair?

O Nancy! when thou'rt far away,
  Wilt thou not cast a wish behind?
Say, canst thou face the parching ray,
  Nor shrink before the wintry wind?
O can that soft and gentle mien,
  Extremes of hardship learn to bear,
Nor sad regret each courtly scene,
  Where thou wert fairest of the fair?

O Nancy! canst thou love so true,
  Through perils keen with me to go,
Or when thy swain mishap shall rue,
  To share with him the pang of woe?
Say, should disease or pain befall,
  Wilt thou assume the nurse's care,
Nor wistful those gay scenes recall,
  Where thou wert fairest of the fair?

And when at last thy love shall die,
  Wilt thou receive his parting breath?
Wilt thou repress each struggling sigh,
  And cheer with smiles the bed of death?
And wilt thou o'er his breathless clay
  Strew flowers, and drop the tender tear,
Nor then regret those scenes so gay,
  Where thou wert fairest of the fair?

Thomas Percy.

SALLY IN OUR ALLEY.

Of all the girls that are so smart
  There's none like pretty Sally;
She is the darling of my heart,
  And she lives in our alley.
There is no lady in the land
  Is half so sweet as Sally;
She is the darling of my heart,
  And she lives in our alley.

Her father he makes cabbage-nets,
  And through the streets does cry 'em;
Her mother she sells laces long
  To such as please to buy 'em;
But sure such folks could ne'er beget
  So sweet a girl as Sally!
She is the darling of my heart,
  And she lives in our alley.

When she is by I leave my work,
  I love her so sincerely;
My master comes like any Turk,
  And bangs me most severely.
But let him bang his bellyful—
  I'll bear it all for Sally;
For she's the darling of my heart,
  And she lives in our alley.

Of all the days that's in the week
  I dearly love but one day,
And that's the day that comes betwixt
  The Saturday and Monday;
For then I'm drest all in my best
  To walk abroad with Sally;
She is the darling of my heart,
  And she lives in our alley.

My master carries me to church,
  And often am I blaméd
Because I leave him in the lurch
  As soon as text is naméd:
I leave the church in sermon-time,
  And slink away to Sally,—
She is the darling of my heart,
  And she lives in our alley.

When Christmas comes about again,
  O then I shall have money!
I'll hoard it up, and box and all,
  I'll give it to my honey;
O, would it were ten thousand pound!
  I'd give it all to Sally;
For she's the darling of my heart,
  And she lives in our alley.

My master and the neighbors all
  Make game of me and Sally,
And but for her I'd better be
  A slave, and row a galley;
But when my seven long years are out,
  O then I'll marry Sally!
O then we'll wed, and then we'll bed—
  But not in our alley!

Harry Carey.

BLACK-EYED SUSAN.

ALL in the Downs the fleet was moor'd,
  The streamers waving in the wind,
When black-eyed Susan came on board,
  "Oh, where shall I my true-love find?
Tell me, ye jovial sailors, tell me true,
Does my sweet William sail among your crew?"

William, who high upon the yard
  Rock'd by the billows to and fro,
Soon as the well-known voice he heard,
  He sigh'd and cast his eyes below;
The cord flies swiftly through his glowing hands,
And, quick as lightning, on the deck he stands.

So the sweet lark, high poised in air,
  Shuts close his pinions to his breast
If chance his mate's shrill call he hear,
  And drops at once into her nest:—
The noblest captain in the British fleet
Might envy William's lip those kisses sweet.

"O Susan, Susan, lovely dear,
  My vows shall ever true remain;
Let me kiss off that falling tear;
  We only part to meet again.
Change as ye list, ye winds; my heart shall be
The faithful compass that still points to thee.

"Believe not what the landsmen say
  Who tempt with doubts thy constant mind:
They'll tell thee, sailors, when away,
  In every port a mistress find:
Yes, yes, believe them when they tell thee so,
For Thou art present wheresoe'er I go."

The boatswain gave the dreadful word,
  The sails their swelling bosom spread;
No longer must she stay aboard;
  They kiss'd, she sigh'd, he hung his head.
Her lessening boat unwilling rows to land;
"Adieu!" she cries; and waves her lily hand.

J. Gay.

YE GENTLEMEN OF ENGLAND.

YE gentlemen of England
  That live at home at ease,
Ah! little do you think upon
  The dangers of the seas.
Give ear unto the mariners,
  And they will plainly shew
All the cares and the fears
  When the stormy winds do blow.

If enemies oppose us
  When England is at war
With any foreign nation,
  We fear not wound or scar;
Our roaring guns shall teach 'cm
  Our valour for to know,
Whilst they reel on the keel,
  And the stormy winds do blow.

Then courage, all brave mariners,
  And never be dismay'd;
While we have bold adventurers,
  We ne'er shall want a trade:
Our merchants will employ us
  To fetch them wealth, we know;
Then be bold—work for gold,
  When the stormy winds do blow.

Martyn Parker.

TO ALL YOU LADIES NOW ON LAND.

To all you ladies now on land,
  We men at sea indite;
But first would have you understand
  How hard it is to write:
The muses now, and Neptune, too,
We must implore to write to you.
              With a fa, la, la, la, la.

For though the muses should prove kind,
  And fill our empty brain;
Yet if rough Neptune rouse the wind,
  To wave the azure main,
Our paper, pen, and ink, and we,
Roll up and down in ships at sea.
              With a fa, la, la, la, la.

Then if we write not by each post,
  Think not we are unkind;
Nor yet conclude our ships are lost
  By Dutchmen or by wind:
Our tears we'll send a speedier way—
The tide shall bring them twice a day.
              With a fa, la, la, la, la.

The king, with wonder and surprise,
  Will swear the seas grow bold;
Because the tides will higher rise
  Than e'er they did of old:
But let him know it is our tears
Bring floods of grief to Whitehall-stairs.
       With a fa, la, la, la, la.

Should foggy Opdam chance to know
  Our sad and dismal story,
The Dutch would scorn so weak a foe,
  And quit their fort at Goree:
For what resistance can they find
From men who've left their hearts behind?
       With a fa, la, la, la, la.

Let wind and weather do its worst,
  Be ye to us but kind;
Let Dutchmen vapour, Spaniards curse,
  No sorrow shall we find:
'Tis then no matter how things go,
Or who's our friend, or who's our foe.
       With a fa, la, la, la, la.

To pass our tedious hours away,
  We throw a merry main,
Or else at serious ombre play;
  But why should we in vain
Each other's ruin thus pursue?
We were undone when we left you.
       With a fa, la, la, la, la.

But now our fears tempestuous grow,
  And cast our hopes away;
Whilst you, regardless of our woe,
  Sit careless at a play;
Perhaps permit some happier man
To kiss your hand, or flirt your fan.
          With a fa, la, la, la, la.

When any mournful tune you hear
  That dies in ev'ry note,
As if it sighed with each man's care,
  For being so remote:
Then think how often love we've made
To you, when all those tunes were play'd!
          With a fa, la, la, la, la.

In justice you cannot refuse
  To think of our distress,
When we, for hopes of honour, lose
  Our certain happiness!
All those designs are but to prove
Ourselves more worthy of your love!
          With a fa, la, la, la, la.

And now we've told you all our loves,
  And likewise all our fears;
In hopes this declaration moves
  Some pity for our tears;
Let's hear of no inconstancy—
We have too much of that at sea.
          With a fa, la, la, la, la.

                    Charles Sackville, Lord Dorset.

THE LOSS OF THE ROYAL GEORGE.

TOLL for the Brave!
The brave that are no more!
All sunk beneath the wave
Fast by their native shore!

Eight hundred of the brave
Whose courage well was tried,
Had made the vessel heel
And laid her on her side.

A land-breeze shook the shrouds
And she was overset;
Down went the Royal George,
With all her crew complete.

Toll for the brave!
Brave Kempenfelt is gone;
His last sea-fight is fought,
His work of glory done.

It was not in the battle;
No tempest gave the shock;
She sprang no fatal leak,
She ran upon no rock.

His sword was in its sheath,
His fingers held the pen,
When Kempenfelt went down
With twice four hundred men.

Weigh the vessel up
Once dreaded by our foes!
And mingle with our cup
The tear that England owes.

Her timbers yet are sound,
And she may float again
Full charged with England's thunder,
And plough the distant main:

But Kempenfelt is gone,
His victories are o'er;
And he and his eight hundred
Shall plough the wave no more.

W. Cowper.

THE DEATH OF THE BRAVE.

How sleep the brave, who sink to rest
By all their country's wishes blest!
When spring, with dewy fingers cold,
Returns to deck their hallow'd mould,
She there shall dress a sweeter sod
Than fancy's feet have ever trod.

By fairy hands their knell is rung,
By forms unseen their dirge is sung:
There Honour comes, a pilgrim grey,
To bless the turf that wraps their clay;
And Freedom shall awhile repair,
To dwell a weeping hermit there.

W. Collins.

A DIRGE.

O SING unto my roundelay,
  O drop the briny tear with me;
Dance no more at holyday,
  Like a running river be:
     My love is dead,
     Gone to his death-bed,
All under the willow-tree.

Black his cryne as the winter night,
  White his rode as the summer snow,
Red his face as the morning light,
  Cold he lies in the grave below:
     My love is dead,
     Gone to his death-bed,
All under the willow-tree.

Sweet his tongue as the throstle's note,
  Quick in dance as thought can be,
Deft his tabor, cudgel stout;
  O! he lies by the willow-tree:
     My love is dead,
     Gone to his death-bed,
All under the willow-tree.

Hark! the raven flaps his wing
  In the brier'd dell below;
Hark! the death-owl loud doth sing
  To the night-mares as they go:
     My love is dead,
     Gone to his death-bed,
All under the willow-tree.

See! the white moon shines on high;
 Whiter is my true love's shroud,
Whiter than the morning sky,
 Whiter than the evening cloud:
  My love is dead,
  Gone to his death-bed,
 All under the willow-tree.

Here upon my true love's grave
 Shall the barren flowers be laid,
Not one holy Saint to save
 All the calness of a maid:
  My love is dead,
  Gone to his death-bed,
 All under the willow-tree.

With my hands I'll dent the briars
 Round his holy corse to gree;
Ouphant fairy, light your fires—
 Here my body still shall be:
  My love is dead,
  Gone to his death-bed,
 All under the willow-tree.

Come, with acorn-cup and thorn,
 Drain my heartè's blood away;
Life and all its goods I scorn,
 Dance by night, or feast by day:
  My love is dead,
  Gone to his death-bed,
 All under the willow tree.

Water-witches crowned with reytes,
 Bear me to your Lethal tide.
I die! I come! my true love waits!
 Thus the damsel spake, and died.

Thomas Chatterton.

YARROW STREAM.

THY banks were bonnie, Yarrow stream,
When first on thee I met my lover;
Thy banks how dreary, Yarrow stream,
When now thy waves his body cover!

For ever now, O Yarrow stream,
Thou art to me a stream of sorrow;
For never on thy banks shall I
Behold my love—the flower of Yarrow!

He promised me a milk-white horse,
To bear me to his father's bowers;
He promised me a little page,
To squire me to his father's towers.

He promised me a wedding-ring,
The wedding-day was fixed to-morrow;
Now he is wedded to his grave,
Alas! a watery grave in Yarrow!

Sweet were his words when last we met;
My passion as I freely told him;
Clasp'd in his arms, I little thought
That I should never more behold him.

Scarce was he gone, I saw his ghost—
It vanished with a shriek of sorrow;
Thrice did the Water Wraith ascend,
And give a doleful groan through Yarrow!

His mother from the window looked,
With all the longing of a mother;
His little sister, weeping, walked
The greenwood path to meet her brother.

They sought him east, they sought him west
They sought him all the forest thorough;
They only saw the clouds of night—
They only heard the roar of Yarrow!

No longer from thy window look—
Thou hast no son, thou tender mother!
No longer walk, thou lovely maid—
Alas! thou hast no more a brother!

No longer seek him east or west,
No longer search the forest thorough,
For, murdered in the night so dark,
He lies a lifeless corpse in Yarrow!

The tears shall never leave my cheek
No other youth shall be my marrow;
I'll seek thy body in the stream,
And there with thee I'll sleep in Yarrow!

The tear did never leave her cheek,
No other youth became her marrow;
She found his body in the stream,
And with him now she sleeps in Yarrow.

J. Logan.

BONNIE GEORGE CAMPBELL.

SCOTTISH BALLAD.

High upon Highlands,
  And low upon Tay,
Bonnie George Campbell
  Rode out on a day,
Saddled and bridled,
  And gallant to see;
Hame cam' his gude horse,
  But hame came not he.

Out ran his auld mither,
  Greeting full sair;
Out ran his bonnie bride
  Reaving her hair.
He rode saddled and bridled,
  Wi' boots to the knee:
Hame cam' his gude horse
  But never cam' he.

"My meadow lies green,
  And my corn is unshorn,
My barn is unbuilt,
  And my babe is unborn!"
He rode saddled and bridled,
  Careless and free:
Hame cam' his gude horse,
  And never cam' he.

Anonymous.

LOVE'S LAMENTATION.

O WALY waly up the bank,
  And waly waly down the brae,
And waly waly yon burn-side
  Where I and my Love were wont to gae!
I leant my back unto an aik,
  I thought it was a trusty tree;
But first it bow'd and syne it brake,
  Sae my true Love did lichtly me.

O waly waly, but love be bonny
  A little time while it is new;
But when 'tis auld, it waxeth cauld
  And fades awa' like morning dew.
O wherefore should I busk my head?
  Or wherefore should I kame my hair?
For my true Love has me forsook,
  And says he'll never loe me mair.

Now Arthur-seat sall be my bed;
  The sheets shall ne'er be prest by me:
Saint Anton's well sall be my drink,
  Since my true Love has forsaken me.
Marti'mas wind, when wilt thou blaw
  And shake the green leaves aff the tree?
O gentle Death, when wilt thou come?
  For of my life I am wearie.

'Tis not the frost that freezes fell,
  Nor blawing snaw's inclemencie;
'Tis not sic cauld that makes me cry,
  But my Love's heart grown cauld to me.
When we came in by Glasgow town
  We were a comely sight to see;
My Love was clad in the black velvét,
  And I mysell in cramasie.

But had I wist, before I kist,
  That love had been sae ill to win;
I had lockt my heart in a case of gowd
  And pinn'd it with a siller pin.
And, O! if my young babe were born,
  And set upon the nurse's knee,
And I mysell were dead and gane,
  And the green grass growing over me!

Anonymous.

AULD ROBIN GRAY.

WHEN the sheep are in the fauld and the kye's come hame,
And a' the weary warld to rest are gane,
The waes o' my heart fa' in showers frae my e'e,
Unkent by my gudeman, wha sleeps sound by me.

Young Jamie lo'ed me weel and sought me for his bride,
But saving ae crown-piece he had naething beside;
To make the crown a pound my Jamie gaed to sea,
And the crown and the pound, they were baith for me.

He hadna been gane a twelvemonth and a day,
When my father brake his arm and the cow was stown away;
My mither she fell sick—my Jamie was at sea,
And auld Robin Gray came a courting me.

My father couldna wark—my mother couldna spin—
I toiled night and day, but their bread I couldna win;
Auld Rob maintained them baith, and wi' tears in his e'e,
Said, "Jeanie, for their sakes, will ye no marry me?"

My heart it said na, and I looked for Jamie back,
But hard blew the winds, and his ship it was a wrack;
His ship was a wrack—why didna Jamie die,
Or why am I spared to cry wae is me?

My father urged me sair—my mither didna speak,
But she looked in my face till my heart was like to break;
They gied him my hand— my heart was in the sea—
And so auld Robin Gray he was gudeman to me.

I hadna been his wife a week but only four,
When, mournfu' I sat on the stane at my door,
I saw my Jamie's ghaist—for I couldna think it he—
Till he said "I'm come hame, my love, to marry thee!"

Oh, sair, sair did me greet, and mickle say of a',
I gied him ae kiss, and bade him gang awa'—
I wist that I were dead, but I'm na like to die,
For though my heart is broken, I'm but young, wae is me!

I gang like a ghaist, and I carena much to spin,
I darena think o' Jamie, for that would be a sin;
But I'll do my best a gude wife to be
To auld Robin Gray, for he is kind to me.

Lady Anne Barnard.

TO MARY UNWIN.

THE twentieth year is well nigh past
Since first our sky was overcast;
Ah would that this might be the last!
    My Mary!

Thy spirits have a fainter flow,
I see thee daily weaker grow—
'Twas my distress that brought thee low,
    My Mary!

Thy needles, once a shining store,
For my sake restless heretofore,
Now rust disused, and shine no more;
    My Mary!

For though thou gladly wouldst fulfil
The same kind office for me still,
Thy sight now seconds not thy will,
    My Mary!

But well thou play'dst the housewife's part,
And all thy threads with magic art
Have wound themselves about this heart,
    My Mary!

Thy indistinct expressions seem
Like language utter'd in a dream;
Yet me they charm, whate'er the theme,
    My Mary!

Thy silver locks, once auburn bright,
Are still more lovely in my sight
Than golden beams of orient light,
    My Mary!

For could I view nor them nor thee,
What sight worth seeing could I see?
The sun would rise in vain for me,
    My Mary!

Partakers of thy sad decline
Thy hands their little force resign;
Yet gently press'd, press gently mine,
    My Mary!

Such feebleness of limbs thou prov'st
That now at every step thou mov'st
Upheld by two; yet still thou lov'st,
    My Mary!

And still to love, though press'd with ill,
In wintry age to feel no chill,
With me is to be lovely still,
    My Mary!

But ah! by constant heed I know
How oft the sadness that I show
Transforms thy smiles to looks of woe,
    My Mary!

And should my future lot be cast
With much resemblance of the past,
Thy worn-out heart will break at last—
    My Mary!

W. Cowper.

TO THE MUSES.

WHETHER on Ida's shady brow,
  Or in the chambers of the East,
The chambers of the Sun, that now
  From ancient melody have ceased;

Whether in heaven ye wander fair,
  Or the green corners of the earth,
Or the blue regions of the air
  Where the melodious winds have birth;

Whether on crystal rocks ye rove
  Beneath the bosom of the sea,
Wandering in many a coral grove,
  Fair Nine, forsaking Poetry;

How have you left the ancient love
  That bards of old enjoyed in you!
The languid strings do scarcely move,
  The sound is forced, the notes are few!

W. Blake.

ALEXANDER'S FEAST,

AN ODE IN HONOUR OF ST. CECILIA'S DAY.

'TWAS at the royal feast for Persia won
    By Philip's warlike son:
Aloft in awful state
The godlike hero sate
    On his imperial throne:
His valiant peers were placed around;
Their brows with roses and with myrtle bound,
    (So should desert in arms be crown'd):
The lovely Thaïs by his side
Sate, like a blooming Eastern bride,
In flower of youth and beauty's pride.
    Happy, happy, happy pair!
    None but the brave,
    None but the brave,
    None but the brave deserves the fair.

Timotheus, placed on high
    Amid the tuneful quire,
    With flying fingers touch'd the lyre:
The trembling notes ascend the sky,
    And heavenly joys inspire.
The song began from Jove,
Who left his blissful seats above
(Such is the power of mighty Love!).

A dragon's fiery form belied the god,
Sublime on radiant spheres he rode,
      When he to fair Olympia press'd,
And stamp'd an image of himself, a sovereign of the world.

The listening crowd admire the lofty sound,
A present deity! they shout around:
A present deity! the vaulted roofs rebound:
            With ravish'd ears
            The monarch hears,
            Assumes the god,
            Affects to nod,
And seems to shake the spheres.

The praise of Bacchus then the sweet musician sung:
   Of Bacchus ever fair and ever young:
      The jolly god in triumph comes;
      Sound the trumpets, beat the drums;
         Flush'd with a purple grace,
         He shows his honest face;
Now give the hautboys breath: he comes! he comes!
      Bacchus, ever fair and young,
      Drinking joys did first ordain;
      Bacchus' blessings are a treasure,
      Drinking is the soldier's pleasure:
            Rich the treasure,
            Sweet the pleasure;
      Sweet is pleasure after pain.

      Soothed with the sound, the king grew vain;
      Fought all his battles o'er again;
And thrice he routed all his foes, and thrice he slew the slain.
The master saw the madness rise,
His glowing cheeks, his ardent eyes:
And while he Heaven and Earth defied,
Changed his hand and check'd his pride.

He chose a mournful Muse
Soft pity to infuse:
He sung Darius great and good,
By too severe a fate
Fallen, fallen, fallen, fallen,
Fallen from his high estate,
And weltering in his blood;
Deserted at his utmost need
By those his former bounty fed,
On the bare earth exposed he lies
With not a friend to close his eyes.
—With downcast looks the joyless victor sate,
Revolving in his alter'd soul
The various turns of Chance below;
And now and then a sigh he stole,
And tears began to flow.

The mighty master smiled to see
That love was in the next degree;
'Twas but a kindred sound to move,
For pity melts the mind to love.
Softly sweet, in Lydian measures
Soon he soothed his soul to pleasures.
War, he sung, is toil and trouble,
Honour but an empty bubble,
Never ending, still beginning;
Fighting still, and still destroying;
If the world be worth thy winning,
Think, O think, it worth enjoying:
Lovely Thais sits beside thee,
Take the good the gods provide thee!
—The many rend the skies with loud applause;
So Love was crown'd, but Music won the cause.
The prince, unable to conceal his pain,
Gazed on the fair
Who caused his care,

And sigh'd and look'd, sigh'd and look'd,
Sigh'd and look'd, and sigh'd again:
At length, with love and wine at once opprest,
The vanquish'd victor sunk upon her breast.

Now strike the golden lyre again:
A louder yet, and yet a louder strain!
Break his bands of sleep asunder
And rouse him like a rattling peal of thunder.
Hark, hark! the horrid sound
Has raised up his head:
As awaked from the dead
And amazed he stares around.
Revenge, revenge, Timotheus cries,
See the Furies arise!
See the snakes that they rear
How they hiss in their hair,
And the sparkles that flash from their eyes!
Behold a ghastly band
Each a torch in his hand!
Those are Grecian ghosts, that in battle were slain
And unburied remain
Inglorious on the plain:
Give the vengeance due
To the valiant crew!
Behold how they toss their torches on high,
How they point to the Persian abodes
And glittering temples of their hostile gods.
—The princes applaud with a furious joy:
And the King seized a flambeau with zeal to destroy;
Thais led the way
To light him to his prey,
And like another Helen, fired another Troy!

Thus, long ago,
Ere heaving bellows learn'd to blow,

While organs yet were mute;
Timotheus to his breathing flute
And sounding lyre,
Could swell the soul to rage, or kindle soft desire.
At last divine Cecilia came,
Inventress of the vocal frame;
The sweet enthusiast, from her sacred store,
Enlarged the former narrow bounds,
And added length to solemn sounds,
With Nature's mother-wit, and arts unknown before.
Let old Timotheus yield the prize,
Or both divide the crown;
He raised a mortal to the skies,
She drew an angel down.

John Dryden.

ODE ON ST. CECILIA'S DAY.

DESCEND, ye Nine! descend and sing,
The breathing instruments inspire;
Wake into voice each silent string,
And sweep the sounding lyre!
In a sadly pleasing strain
Let the warbling lute complain:
Let the loud trumpet sound,
Till the roofs all around
The shrill echoes rebound:
While in more lengthen'd notes and slow
The deep, majestic, solemn organs blow.
Hark! the numbers soft and clear
Gently steal upon the ear;
Now louder, and yet louder rise,
And fill with spreading sounds the skies;

Exulting in triumph now swell the bold notes,
In broken air, trembling, the wild music floats
    Till, by degrees, remote and small,
        The strains decay,
        And melt away
    In a dying, dying fall.

By Music, minds an equal temper know,
    Not swell too high, nor sink too low;
If in the brief tumultuous joys arise,
Music her soft, assuasive voice applies;
    Or, when the soul is press'd with cares,
    Exalts her in enliv'ning airs:
Warriors she fires with animated sounds,
Pours balm into the bleeding lover's wounds;
        Melancholy lifts her head,
        Morpheus rouses from his bed,
        Sloth unfolds her arms and wakes,
        List'ning Envy drops her snakes,
Intestine war no more our Passions wage,
And giddy Factions hear away their rage.

But when our country's cause provokes to arms,
How martial music ev'ry bosom warms!
So when the first bold vessel dar'd the seas,
High on the stern the Thracian rais'd his strain,
    While Argo saw her kindred trees
    Descend from Pelion to the main,
    Transported demigods stood round,
    And men grew heroes at the sound,
        Inflam'd with glory's charms:
    Each chief his sev'nfold shield display'd,
    And half unsheath'd the shining blade:
    And seas, and rock, and skies rebound;
        To arms! to arms! to arms!

But when through all the infernal bounds,
Which flaming Phlegethon surrounds,
    Love, strong as Death, the poet led
    To the pale nations of the dead,
What sounds were heard,
What scenes appear'd,
  O'er all the dreary coasts?
    Dreadful gleams,
    Dismal screams,
    Fires that glow,
    Shrieks of wo,
    Sullen moans,
    Hollow groans,
  And cries of tortured ghosts,
But hark! he strikes the golden lyre;
And see! the tortured ghosts respire,
    See, shady forms advance!
  Thy stone, O Sisyphus, stands still,
  Ixion rests upon his wheel,
    And the pale spectres dance!

The Furies sink upon their iron beds,
And snakes uncurl'd hang list'ning round their heads.
  By the streams that ever flow,
  By the fragrant winds that blow
    O'er th' Elysian flow'rs;
  By those happy souls who dwell
  In yellow meads of asphodel,
    Or amaranthine bow'rs;
  By the heroes' arméd shades,
  Glitt'ring through the gloomy glades,
  By the youths that died for love,
    Wand'ring in the myrtle grove;
Restore, restore Eurydice to life:
O, take the Husband, or return the Wife!

He sung, and Hell consented
  To hear the poet's prayer:
Stern Proserpine relented,
  And gave him back the fair:
    Thus song could prevail
    O'er Death and o'er Hell,
A conquest how hard, and how glorious!
  Though Fate had fast bound her,
  With Styx nine times round her,
Yet Music and Love were victorious.

But soon, too soon, the lover turns his eyes,
Again she falls—again she dies—she dies!
How wilt thou now the fatal sisters move?
No crime was thine, if 'tis no crime to love.
  Now under hanging mountains,
  Beside the falls of fountains,
  Or where Hebrus wanders,
  Rolling in meanders,
    All alone,
    Unheard, unknown,
    He makes his moan;
    And calls her ghost,
  For ever, ever, ever lost!
  Now with Furies surrounded,
  Despairing, confounded,
  He trembles, he glows,
  Amidst Rhodope's snows:
See, wild as the winds, o'er the desert he flies;
Hark! Hæmus resounds with the Bacchanals' cries—
    Ah see, he dies!

Yet ev'n in death Eurydice he sung,
Eurydice still trembled on his tongue,
  Eurydice the woods,
  Eurydice the floods,

Eurydice the rocks, and hollow mountains rung.
　　Music the fiercest grief can charm,
　　And fate's severest rage disarm;
　　Music can soften pain to ease,
　　And make despair and madness please;
　　Our joys below it can improve,
　　And antedate the bliss above.
　　This the divine Cecilia found,
And to her Maker's praise confin'd the sound.
When the full organ joins the tuneful quire,
　　Th' immortal pow'rs incline their ear
Borne on the swelling notes our souls aspire,
While solemn airs improve the sacred fire;
　　And angels lean from Heav'n to hear.
Of Orpheus now no more let poets tell,
To bright Cecilia greater pow'r is giv'n;
　　His numbers rais'd a shade from Hell,
　　Hers lift the soul to Heav'n.

A. Pope.

ODE ON THE UNIVERSE.

THE spacious firmament on high,
With all the blue ethereal sky
And spangled heavens (a shining frame)
Their great Original proclaim.
The unwearied sun, from day to day,
Does his Creator's power display,
And publishes to every land
The work of an Almighty hand.
Soon as the evening shades prevail,
The moon takes up the wondrous tale;
And nightly to the listening earth
Repeats the story of her birth;
Whilst all the stars that round her burn,
And all the planets in their turn,
Confirm the tidings, as they roll
And spread the truth from pole to pole.
What, though in solemn silence all
Move round the dark terrestrial ball;
What, though no real voice, nor sound,
Amidst their radiant orbs be found;
In reason's ear they all rejoice,
And utter forth a glorious voice:
For ever singing as they shine:—
"The Hand that made us is divine."

Joseph Addison.

ODE ON THE MORNING OF CHRIST'S NATIVITY.

THIS is the month, and this the happy morn
Wherein the Son of Heaven's Eternal King
Of wedded maid and virgin mother born,
Our great redemption from above did bring;
For so the holy sages once did sing
That he our deadly forfeit should release,
And with his Father work us a perpetual peace.

That glorious Form, that Light unsufferable,
And that far-beaming blaze of Majesty
Wherewith he wont at Heaven's high council-table
To sit the midst of Trinal Unity,
He laid aside; and, here with us to be,
Forsook the courts of everlasting day,
And chose with us a darksome house of mortal clay.

Say, heavenly Muse, shall not thy sacred vein
Afford a present to the Infant God?
Hast thou no verse, no hymn, or solemn strain
To welcome him to this his new abode,
Now while the heaven, by the sun's team untrod,
Hath took no print of the approaching light,
And all the spangled host keep watch in squadrons bright?

See how from far, upon the eastern road,
The star-led wizards haste with odours sweet:
O run, prevent them with thy humble ode

And lay it lowly at his blessed feet;
Have thou the honour first thy Lord to greet,
And join thy voice unto the angel quire
From out his secret altar touch'd with hallow'd fire.

THE HYMN.

It was the winter wild
While the heaven-born Child
All meanly wrapt in the rude manger lies;
Nature in awe to him
Had doff'd her gaudy trim,
With her great Master so to sympathize:
It was no season then for her
To wanton with the sun, her lusty paramour.

Only with speeches fair
She woos the gentle air
To hide her guilty front with innocent snow;
And on her naked shame,
Pollute with sinful blame,
The saintly veil of maiden white to throw;
Confounded, that her Maker's eyes
Should look so near upon her foul deformities.

But he, her fears to cease,
Sent down the meek-eyed Peace;
She, crown'd with olive green, came softly sliding
Down through the turning sphere,
His ready harbinger,
With turtle wing the amorous clouds dividing;
And waving wide her myrtle wand,
She strikes a universal peace through sea and land.

No war, or battle's sound
Was heard the world around:

The idle spear and shield were high up hung;
The hookéd chariot stood
Unstain'd with hostile blood;
The trumpet spake not to the arméd throng;
And kings sat still with awful eye,
As if they surely knew their sovran Lord was by.

But peaceful was the night
Wherein the Prince of Light
His reign of peace upon the earth began:
The winds, with wonder whist,
Smoothly the waters kist
Whispering new joys to the mild oceán—
Who now hath quite forgot to rave,
While birds of calm sit brooding on the charméd wave.

The stars, with deep amaze,
Stand fix'd in stedfast gaze,
Bending one way their precious influence;
And will not take their flight
For all the morning light,
Or Lucifer that often warn'd them thence;
But in their glimmering orbs did glow
Until their Lord himself bespake, and bid them go.

And though the shady gloom
Had given day her room,
The sun himself withheld his wonted speed,
And hid his head for shame,
As his inferior flame
The new-enlighten'd world no more should need:
He saw a greater Sun appear
Than his bright throne, or burning axletree, could bear.

The shepherds on the lawn
Or ere the point of dawn

Sate simply chatting in a rustic row;
Full little thought they then
That the mighty Pan
Was kindly come to live with them below;
Perhaps their loves, or else their sheep
Was all that did their silly thoughts so busy keep.

When such music sweet
Their hearts and ears did greet
As never was by mortal finger strook—
Divinely-warbled voice
Answering the stringéd noise,
As all their souls in blissful rapture took:
The air, such pleasure loth to lose,
With thousand echoes still prolongs each heavenly close.

Nature that heard such sound
Beneath the hollow round
Of Cynthia's seat the aery region thrilling,
Now was almost won
To think her part was done,
And that her reign had here its last fulfilling;
She knew such harmony alone
Could hold all heaven and earth in happier union.

At last surrounds their sight
A globe of circular light
That with long beams the shamefaced night array'd;
The helméd Cherubim
And sworded Seraphim
Are seen in glittering ranks with wings display'd,
Harping in loud and solemn quire
With unexpressive notes, to Heaven's new-born Heir.

Such music (as 'tis said)
Before was never made

But when of old the sons of morning sung,
While the Creator great
His constellations set
And the well-balanced world on hinges hung;
And cast the dark foundations deep,
And bid the weltering waves their oozy channel keep.

Ring out, ye crystal spheres!
Once bless our human ears,
If ye have power to touch our senses so;
And let your silver chime
Move in melodious time;
And let the base of heaven's deep organ blow;
And with your ninefold harmony
Make up full conceit to the angelic symphony.

For if such holy song
Enwrap our fancy long,
Time will run back, and fetch the age of gold;
And speckled vanity
Will sicken soon and die,
And leprous sin will melt from earthly mould;
And Hell itself will pass away,
And leave her dolorous mansions to the peering day.

Yea, Truth and Justice then
Will down return to men,
Orb'd in a rainbow; and, like glories wearing,
Mercy will sit between
Throned in celestial sheen,
With radiant feet the tissued clouds down steering;
And Heaven, as at some festival,
Will open wide the gates of her high palace hall.

But wisest Fate says No;
This must not yet be so;

The Babe yet lies in smiling infancy
That on the bitter cross
Must redeem our loss;
So both himself and us to glorify:
Yet first, to those ychain'd in sleep
The wakeful trump of doom must thunder through the deep;

With such a horrid clang
As on mount Sinai rang
While the red fire and smouldering clouds outbrake:
The aged Earth aghast
With terror of that blast
Shall from the surface to the centre shake,
When, at the world's last session,
The dreadful Judge in middle air shall spread his throne.

And then at last our bliss
Full and perfect is,
But now begins; for from this happy day
The old Dragon, under ground
In straiter limits bound,
Not half so far casts his usurpéd sway;
And, wroth to see his kingdom fail,
Swindges the scaly horrour of his folded tail.

The oracles are dumb;
No voice or hideous hum
Runs through the archéd roof in words deceiving:
Apollo from his shrine
Can no more divine,
With hollow shriek the steep of Delphos leaving:
No nightly trance or breathéd spell
Inspires the pale-eyed priest from the prophetic cell.

The lonely mountains o'er
And the resounding shore

A voice of weeping heard, and loud lament;
From haunted spring and dale
Edged with poplar pale
The parting Genius is with sighing sent;
With flower-inwoven tresses torn
The nymphs in twilight shade of tangled thickets mourn.

In consecrated earth
And on the holy hearth
The Lars and Lemurés moan with midnight plaint;
In urns, and altars round
A drear and dying sound
Affrights the Flamens at their service quaint;
And the chill marble seems to sweat,
While each peculiar Power foregoes his wonted seat.

Peor and Baalim
Forsake their temples dim,
With that twice-batter'd god of Palestine;
And moonéd Ashtaroth
Heaven's queen and mother both,
Now sits not girt with tapers' holy shine;
The Lybic Hammon shrinks his horn,
In vain the Tyrian maids their wounded Thammuz mourn.

And sullen Moloch, fled,
Hath left in shadows dread
His burning idol all of blackest hue;
In vain with cymbals' ring
They call the grisly king,
In dismal dance about the furnace blue;
The brutish gods of Nile as fast
Isis, and Orus, and the dog Anubis, haste.

Nor is Osiris seen
In Memphian grove, or green,

Trampling the unshower'd grass with lowings loud;
Nor can he be at rest
Within his sacred chest;
Nought but profoundest hell can be his shroud;
In vain with timbrell'd anthems dark
The sable stoléd sorcerers bear his worshipt ark.

He feels from Juda's land
The dreaded infant's hand;
The rays of Bethlehem blind his dusky eyn;   .
Nor all the gods beside
Longer dare abide,
Nor Typhon huge ending in snaky twine:
Our Babe, to show his Godhead true,
Can in his swaddling bands control the damnéd crew.

So, when the sun in bed
Curtain'd with cloudy red
Pillows his chin upon an orient wave,
The flocking shadows pale
Troop to the infernal jail,
Each fetter'd ghost slips to his several grave;
And the yellow-skirted fays
Fly after the night-steeds, leaving their moon-loved maze.

But see, the Virgin blest
Hath laid her Babe to rest;
Time is, our tedious song should here have ending:
Heaven's youngest-teeméd star
Hath fixed her polish'd car,
Her sleeping Lord with hand-maid lamp attending:
And all about the courtly stable
Bright-harness'd angels sit in order serviceable.

J. Milton.

18*

NOTES.

Page 3. "LOVE-LONGING." One of the very few English love-songs extant of so early a period. Campbell, selecting it as a specimen of thirteenth century versification, observes that "such a stanza would not disgrace the lyric poetry of a refined age." Line 4. *wex*—wax. L. 5. *in sleep I slake*—am deprived of sleep.

Page 3. "RONDEAU"—*G. Chaucer*. This little ballad was printed for the first time by Bishop Percy (see 'Reliques') from a MS. in the Pepysian Library. "The versification," he remarks, "is of that species which the French call Rondeau; very naturally Englished by our honest countrymen, Round O. Though so early adopted by them, our ancestors had not the honour of inventing it. Chaucer picked it up, along with other better things, among the neighbouring nations." Line 1. *sle*—slay. L. 3. *wendeth*—goeth. L. 4. *helen*—heal. L. 8 *quene*—Queen. L. 11. *pleyn*—complain. L. 12. *cheyne*—chain. L. 14. *soth*—sooth. L. 14. *fayn*—feign. L. 18. *peyn*—pain. L. 20. *ben*—be. L. 20. *lene*—lean. L. 21. *fre*--free. L. 21. *bene*—boon. L. 23. *fors*—force. L. 25. *sclat*—state. L. 26. *clene*—clean. L. 27. *For ever mo*—for evermore. L. 27. *mene*—means.

Page 5. "TO LIFE'S PILGRIM"—*G. Chaucer*. The original contains three verses, of which the second is here omitted; the poem being given merely as a specimen of early versification. Stanza I. Line 1. *press*—crowd. L. 3. *hoard*—treasure. L. 3. *climbing tickleness*—means that advancement is beset with uncertainty. L. 4. *preise*—praise. L. 5. *Savor*—desire. L. 6. *Rede*—counsel. L. 7. *'tis no drede*—there is no cause for fear. Stanza II. L. 1. *That thee is sent receive in buxomness*—that which is sent to thee, receive cheerfully. L. 6. *Weivith thy lust*—subdue thy desires. L. 6. *ghost*—spirit.

Page 5. "TO MAISTRES MARGARETE"—*J. Skelton*. There is a musical lilt in the versification of this little complimentary poem rarely found in the productions of this period. Skelton was author of the famous "Boke of Colin Clout" and of some of the early moralities. Southey says, alluding to his political and satirical writings. "the power, the strangeness, the volubility of his language, the intrepidity of his satire, and the perfect originality of his manner, render Skelton one of the most extraordinary poets of any age or country." The present poem was addressed to one Mistress Margaret Hussey.

Verse 2. Line 3. *fayre Isiphill*—fair Isabel, probably some amous beauty of the day. L. 5. *Swete Pomaunder*—a ball of perfumes used in the toilette of a sixteenth century belle; from the French *pomme d'ambre*. L. 10. *Erst*—ere.

Page 7. "MY SWETE SWETYNG." Tempo Henry VIII; author unknown. "*Pigsnye*" is a term of endearment derived from the old Saxon word *piga*, or girl.

Page 8. "A CAROL OF SPRING"—*H. Howard, Earl of Surrey*. Line 1. *soote*—sweet. L. 11. *mings*—mixes.

Page 8. "MADRIGAL"—*James I. (of Scotland)*. From the beautiful poem entitled "*The King's Quair,*" (i. e. The King's Book) in which he describes his captivity in Windsor Castle and his passion for the Lady Jane Beaufort, whom he afterwards married. James I. perished by assassination in the forty-fourth year of his age. A.D. 1473.

Page 10. "THE PASSIONATE SHEPHERD"—*C. Marlowe*. This elegant little poem belongs to that school of Euphuistic Pastoral of which Sir P. Sidney's *Arcadia* is the most elaborate specimen. Mr. Palgrave observes that "it would be ludicrous to criticise it on the ground of the unshepherdlike or unreal character of some images suggested."—Notes to *Golden Treasury*.

Page 13. "SAMELA"—*fancies* is here conjecturally substituted for "fancy"—Line 11.

Page 14. "To HIS LADY"—*T. Carew*. An exquisite specimen of the Elizabethan school of love-poetry: an elaborate and ornate school founded on the still more elaborate and ornate style of Petrarch and his contemporaries.

Page 18. "THE LOVER GROWETH OLD"—*W. Shakespeare*. The necessity of maintaining a uniform plan has compelled the Editor to prefix titles to this and the two following Sonnets, as well as to others by the same immortal hand. These titles, such as they are, are offered reluctantly, and with diffidence.

Page 22. "THE NIGHTINGALE"—*R. Barnefield*. The *motif* of this charming little poem (set to music in later days by Sir Henry Bishop) is founded on an old Greek legend related by Ovid—Met. VI. 565. Pandion, King of Attica, having appealed for military aid to Tereus, King of the Thracians in Daulis, bestowed upon this ally the hand of his daughter Procne, who became the mother of a son named Itys, or Itylus. Tereus, however, wearied of Procne, and having fallen in love with her sister Philomena, or Philomela, concealed Procne and spread the report of her death. Philomela, however, discovered his treachery; but having been deprived of her tongue by Tereus, in the fear that she should betray him, conveyed the truth to Procne by means of certain words woven into the pattern of a peplum. Procne, in her despair and rage, then slew her young son; served up his flesh to Tereus in a dish; and fled with Philomela. Being pursued by Tereus, the sisters prayed to the gods to change them into birds; and Procne was accordingly transformed into a swallow, and Philomela into a nightingale. The story, however, is told somewhat differently by Pausanias and others, who maintain that the sisters wept themselves to death in Attica, whither they escaped, and that Tereus killed himself in Megara. The cry "Tereu, tereu!" is an ingenious invention of the poet, and besides being an adaptation of the name of Tereus, is curiously like one of the notes of the nightingale. See "*Itylus*," by A. C. Swinburne, in our "*Poetry-Book of Modern Poets.*"

Page 24. "THE LOVER'S APPEAL"—*Sir T. Wyatt.* Line 4. *Grame*—sorrow.

Page 26. "TO THE MOON"—*Sir P. Sidney.* This beautiful Sonnet is marred by the awkward inversion in the last line. The poet means to say "do they there call ungratefulness, virtue?"

Page 28. "TO HIS LUTE"—*W. Drummond.* Line 4. *ramage*, the *wood*-song, or wild-song of an untamed bird; from the French *ramage*. See *Richardson's Dictionary.* In this charming Sonnet we find the germ of an idea afterwards developed by Shelley in his *Lines sent with a guitar.*

Page 30. "LAMENT FOR ASTROPHEL"—*E. Spenser.* This poem (entitled in Spenser's collected works "The Dolefull Lay of Clorinda") has by some critics been attributed to Mary Countess of Pembroke, sister to Sir Philip Sidney. The poem, however, bears the impress of Spenser's hand throughout. See particularly the seventh and eighth verses, closely imitated by Shelley in his "Adonais" more than two hundred and forty years later. The Editor has ventured to omit six verses which form no part of the Lament, and serve only to link the poem with others which precede and follow it. Astrophel is the pastoral name given by the poet to his friend Sir Philip Sidney, who died of a wound received at the Battle of Zutphen, Oct. 17th, 1586.

Page 33. "THE SHEPHERD'S ELEGY"—*W. Browne.* Written in memory of his friend Mr. Thomas Manwood. This elegy is supposed to have suggested to Milton the form of his Lycidas.

Page 35. "LYCIDAS"—*J. Milton.* The Lycidas in memory of whom this elegy was penned, was one Mr. Edward King (a college friend of the poet), who was drowned in 1637 between Chester and the coast of Ireland. "The material structure of this glorious poem," says Mr. Palgrave, "is partly derived from Italian models." Line 15. "*The sisters of the sacred well*—the Muses, whose favorite haunt was supposed to be the fountain of Helicon on Mount Parnassus. L. 36. *Damoetas*, an allusion to some friend, figured under a pastoral name. L. 54. *Mona*—the isle of Anglesea, formerly densely wooded, and a chief residence (according to Selden) of the Druids. L. 55. *Deva*—the river Dee, long the ancient boundary between England and Wales, and the scene of numerous traditions. This river, and the neighbouring island are introduced because near the scene of the shipwreck. L. 58. *The Muse herself that Orpheus bore.* Orpheus was son of the Muse Calliope. He was torn to pieces by the Thracian women, who flung his head into the Hebrus, a river of Thrace, whence it was carried out to sea. His fate was thus indicated by Milton in allusion to that of his lost friend. L. 68 and 69. *Amaryllis and Neæra*—fanciful names for imaginary shepherdesses. L. 75. *The blind Fury*—Atropos, the Fate who severs the thread of human life. L. 85. *O fountain Arethuse*—a fountain in the island of Ortygia, near Syracuse. The nymph of this fountain is reckoned by Virgil (Eclogue IV.) among the nymphs of Sicily, and as the one who inspired pastoral poetry. *Mincius*—named in the next line, is an Italian stream which flows through the Lake of Garda and joins the Po near Mantua. L. 96. *Hippotades*—a name for Æolus; see the Odyssey of

Homer, where it is frequently used. L. 99. *"sleek Panope"*—a Nereid. Mr. Palgrave's note upon this passage is so lucid and scholarly that the Editor ventures to quote it entire. "The names of local deities in the Hellenic mythology express generally some feature in the natural landscape, which the Greeks studied and analysed with their usual unequalled insight and feeling. *Panope* represents the boundlessness of the ocean-horizon when seen from a height, as compared with the limited horizon of the land in hilly countries such as Greece or Asia Minor."—Notes to *The Golden Treasury*. L. 103. *Camus*—the river Cam; Mr. King having been a student in the University of Cambridge. L. 106. *that sanguine flower inscribed with woe*—the ancient poetical hyacinth, which, according to Professor Martyn on Virgil's Eclogues, is the Turkscap lily, the markings of which resemble the characters of the Greek cry of woe, "AI-AI." The idea is borrowed by Milton from Moschus, who says in his elegy to Bion—*Νῦγ, ὑάκινϑε, λάλει τὰ σὰ γράμματα, καὶ πλέον αἴ αἴ Βάμβαλε σοῖς πετάλοισι.*—"Now, hyacinth, more than ever say Ai, Ai, and proclaim your inscribed sorrows!" L. 109. *the pilot of the Galilean lake*—St. Peter, the fisherman of Galilee and doorkeeper of Heaven. L. 128. *the grim wolf*—the Papal church. L. 132. *Alpheus*—a stream of Arcady which appears and disappears, like our river Mole, at various points of its course, and was supposed by the ancients to flow under the sea and join the fountain of Arethusa in Ortygia. The river-god Alpheus, according to the legend, loved and thus pursued the nymph Arethusa. L. 138. *the swart-star*—the dog-star, Sirius. L 159. *moist vows,*—commentators are divided as to the intention of the poet, some interpreting the phrase as tearful vows, *vota lacrymosas*; and others as watery vows, or vows relating to the sea. L. 160. *Bellerus*—a giant personification of Bellerium, the antique name for the Land's End. L. 161. *The great Vision of the Guarded Mount.* The Archangel Michael, the guardian of mariners, is said to have appeared on St. Michael's Mount, Cornwall, as also upon Mont St. Michel, a similar rock lying off the opposite coast of Finisterre. *Namancos and Bayona*, mentioned in the next line, are two places on the coast of Finisterre. Milton here implores the angel to look towards the Irish Channel, and pity the fate of his friend. L. 173. *Him that walked the waves*—a beautiful allusion to the miracle upon lake Tiberias, involving a subtle reference to the temporal loss by sea, and the spiritual salvation of his friend. L. 189. *Doric lay*—Warton observes that "this is a Doric lay because Theocritus and Moschus had respectively written a bucolic elegy on Daphnis and Bion."

Page 42. "A Sea Dirge" followed by "A Land Dirge." The Editor has here followed the sequence and repeated the titles given to these poems by Mr. Palgrave, who also quotes the following well-known criticism of Charles Lamb: "I never saw anything like this funeral dirge, except the ditty which reminds Ferdinand of his drowned father in the Tempest. As that is of the water, watery; so this is of the earth, earthy. Both have that intenseness of feeling which seems to resolve itself into the element which it contemplates."

Page 44. "The Quiet Life"—said to have been written by Pope when he was only twelve years of age.

Page 51. "Life"—*Lord Bacon*. This, together with the five following poems, may be regarded as more or less versions of a well-known Greek epigram attributed by some to Poseidippus and by some to Plato Cornicus. Of the original Greek Mr. J. A. Symonds says, "it may take rank with the most elevated sonnets of modern literature." (*Studies of Greek Poets*, 1st Series, 1873.) The poem here given, by Lord Bacon, is interesting as the work of one who was a "mighty mouthed" master of prose. The figure of the Bubble is a *lieu commun* among Elizabethan writers.

Page 58. "SWEET AND BITTER"—*E. Spenser*. Line 6. *pill*—peel, or husk. L. 8. *sweet is moly*—a fabled herb with fair white blossom, but a black root, said by Homer to have been given to Odysseus by Hermes as a countercharm against the arts of Circe. See Milton :—"That moly
That Hermes once to wise Ulysses gave."

Page 65. "SONG OF THE EMIGRANTS"—*A. Marvel*. This fine fragment is semi-political, semi-polemical, but abounding in rich imaginative colour. The emigrants are fictitious exiles from the intolerant court of Charles I.

Page 72. "THE FAITHLESS SHEPHERD"—*Sir G. Elliot* was father of the first Lord Minto, and held various offices under the crown. He was also distinguished as a Parliamentary orator. He died in 1777. Sir W. Scott warmly admired "*The Faithless Shepherd*," and speaks of it as "that beautiful pastoral song."

Page 73. "WINTER"—*W. Shakespeare*. Line 2. *nail*—a cow-horn. L. 9. *keel*—skim.

Page 76. "A SPRING IDYLL"—*Sir H. Wotton*. This Idyll is introduced by Walton in his 'Complete Angler' with these words—"I do easily believe that peace and patience, and a calm content, did cohabit in the cheerful heart of Sir H. Wotton, because I know that when he was beyond seventy years of age he made this description of a part of the present pleasure that possessed him as he sat quietly, in a summer's evening, on a bank a-fishing."

Page 77. "L'ALLÉGRO"—*J. Milton*. Of this ode and its companion, Mr. Palgrave observes :—"It is a striking proof of Milton's astonishing power, that these, the earliest pure Descriptive Lyrics in our language, should still remain the best in a style which so many great poets have since attempted. The Bright and the Thoughtful aspects of Nature are their subjects; but each is preceded by a mythological introduction in a mixed Classical and Italian manner. The meaning of the first is that Gaiety is the child of Nature; of the second, that Pensiveness is the daughter of Sorrow and Genius."—Notes to *Golden Treasury*. Line 2. *of Cerberus and blackest midnight born*. Some commentators read for Cerberus, Erebus, who according to Hesiod, married with his sister, Night; but the offspring of this union was not Melancholy, but Day and Æther. That Milton wrote and meant Cerberus is sufficiently proved by the allusion to his den, the "Stygian cave," usually placed on the further side of the Styx, at the spot where Charon landed the shades of the dead. L. 10, *Cimmerian*—the mythical Cimmerii of Homer dwelt in the farthest West, on the ocean, enveloped in perpetual mist and darkness. L. 67. *tells his tale*—tale, a technical word for numbering sheep. L. 80. *cynosure*, the polestar, or load-star. L. 132. *Jonson's learned sock*—the sock was a light shoe worn by the Roman comedians, as the buskin by the tragedians. L. 136.

soft Lydian airs—Mr. Palgrave describes the Lydian as "a light and festive style of ancient music." Other commentators assign to it a soft and pathetic character. Milton seems to have conceived of it as sweet and soothing, neither gay nor melancholy.

Page 82. "IL PENSEROSO." Line 18. *Prince Memnon's sister.* Memnon was an apocryphal King of Ethiopia, whom Homer makes an ally of the Trojans. He was the son of Tithonus and Aurora, and was killed by Achilles in revenge for the slaying of Antilochus. By a curious confusion of names, the later Greek travellers gave the name of Memnon to the broken colossus of Amenhotep III. at Thebes (see an able article on *The Statue of Memnon* in No. 276 of the Quarterly Review, April, 1875.) No mention of Memnon's sister occurs in any of the Classic writers; so that, as Dunster observes, "this lady is a creation of the poet." Line 19. *starr'd Ethiop queen*—Cassiope, queen of Ethiopia, who, having incurred the displeasure of the Nereids for claiming to surpass them in beauty, was by Perseus transported to heaven, where she became a constellation. Line 54. *the Cherub contemplation*—the Cherubs were the angels of Knowledge, the Seraphs, of Love. L. 59. *Cynthia*—the moon. Her chariot is sometimes represented drawn by dragons. L. 88. *thrice-great Hermes*—Hermes Trismegistus, the reputed author of a whole system of religious and philosophical literature written by the school of New Platonists, about the 4th century of our era. The New Platonists, identifying the Greek Hermes with the Egyptian Thoth, the patron Deity of Letters, regarded the latter as the original source of all knowledge—in fact as the embodied λόγος— gave to him the name of Trismegistus; and affirmed that he was the teacher of Pythagoras and Plato. Inasmuch as the earliest ethical and religious treatises in the world are those of ancient Egypt, there is a certain basis of truth in this theory. L. 99. *Thebes or Pelops' line*—an allusion to the subject-matter of the tragedies of Æschylus, Sophocles, and Euripides. L. 102. *buskin'd stage*— see note to line 132 of L'Allégro. L. 104. *Musæus*—a poet spoken of by Plato as an actual personage, but supposed by modern commentators to be mythical. L. 109. *him that left half told*—Chaucer, who left his "Squire's Tale" unfinished. Leigh Hunt says: "But why did Milton turn Cambus the Khan in to Cambuscan? The accent in Chaucer is never thrown on the second syllable."—*Imagination and Fancy.* L. 116. *great bards*—Ariosto, Tasso, and Spenser are here alluded to. L. 123. *frounced*—Warton derives this word from the French *froncer*, to curb, wrinkle, or contract. L. 124. *The Attic boy*—Cephalus. L. 134. *Sylvan*, i. e. Silvanus, a Latin deity of woods and groves.

Page 87. "ON MELANCHOLY—*R. Burton.* From that rare old treasure- house of wit, humour, and learning. "The Anatomy of Melancholy." The fifth line of the fifth verse stands in the original "Rare beauties, gallant ladies, shine," which the Editor has, with much diffidence, ventured to print thus— "Rare beauties, gallants, ladies, shine."

Page 89. "MELANCOLIA"—*F. Beaumont.* Leigh Hunt who, with the single exception of Charles Lamb, had perhaps the nicest ear for Elizabethan poetry of any critic who ever lived, attributes these lines to Fletcher. Tradition gives them to Beaumont.

Page 91. "LOVE AND DEATH"—*J. Ford.* From "The Broken Heart." Of his life scarcely any particulars are known. His plays were all published between 1629 and 1639.

Page 92. "SORROW-SONG"—*S. Rowley.* Of this writer we know no more than that he was one of the players in the service of Henry Prince of Wales. He appears in Henslow's list of authors. His best known production is a play called "The Spanish Writer," from which this song is taken.

Page 93. "SLUMBER SONG"—*J. Fletcher.* From *Valentinian*, a joint production of Beaumont and Fletcher. L. Hunt ascribes these verses with great show of probability to Fletcher, certain of the lines being reproduced in his play "An Honest Man's Fortune."

Page 101. "TO APOLLO"—*J. Lylye.* Line 8. *To Physic and to Poesy's king.* Allusion is here made to Apollo as the father of Esculapius. He was also identified in later times with Pæon, the god of the healing art in Homer.

Page 102. "TO BACCHUS"—*F. Beaumont.* Line 1. *Lyæus*—a Roman surname of Bacchus.

Page 103. "HOLIDAY IN ARCADIA"—*J. Shirley.* Lines 13. and 14. *Philomel, leave of Tereus' rape to tell.* See preceding note to "The Nightingale" by R. Barnefield. L. 16. *Thracian lyre*—the lyre of Orpheus, which was given to him by Apollo, and from which he drew sounds so enchanting that the trees on Mount Olympus came down to listen to him.

Page 104. "SONG OF A SATYR"—*J. Fletcher.* From Fletcher's *Faithful Shepherdess.* Mr. Seward traces an imitation (which was possibly unconscious) in this song to Shakespeare's *Song of a Fairy*, (see p. 168;) whereupon Mr. R. Bell remarks, in the notes to his *Songs of the Dramatists*, that "a still closer imitation of Fletcher himself may be found in the *Comus* of Milton, which owes large obligations not only to the imagery and general treatment, but to the plan of the *Faithful Shepherdess.*"

Page 112. "TO ELIZABETH OF BOHEMIA"—*Sir H. Wotton.* Elizabeth, daughter of James I. and Anne of Denmark, married the Elector Palatine, afterwards the unlucky King of Bohemia. From the marriage of her youngest daughter with the Duke of Brunswick we derive the Georges and the Hanoverian line.

Page 113. "THE ROSES IN CASTARA'S BOSOM"—*W. Habington.* This poet, described by Southey as "amiable and irreproachable," addressed all his verses to Castara, the lady whom he apparently courted long, and afterwards happily married. Castara's real name was Lucy, and she was a daughter of W. Herbert, first Lord Powis.

Page 117. "TO ALTHEA"—*Colonel Lovelace.* Written literally in the prison to which he was twice consigned by the Puritan government. Having spent his whole fortune in the Royal cause, he died in great poverty A.D. 1658.

Page 118. "BEAUTY CONCEALED"—*Sir F. Kinaston.* A poem conceived in the costliest strain of hyperbole, at a time when the imagination of poets and speculators alike ran upon spice-islands, corals, pearls, and all the new found riches of the Spanish Main.

Page 121. "SONETTO"—*T. Lodge.* Line 9. *the Muses' quill*—quill is here used in the sense of pipe, as for instance in Lycidas, "he touch'd the tender stops of various quills." L. 11. *weed*—garment.

Page 126. "To HIS LOVE: ON GOING A JOURNEY"—*Dr. Donne.* Professor Craik remarks of this poem that "somewhat fantastic as it may be thought, it is notwithstanding full of feeling, and nothing can be more delicate than the execution."

Page 128. "To LUCASTA"—*Col. Lovelace.* Lucasta is said to have been a Miss Lucy Sacheverel, who, hearing a false report of his death when gone "to the Wars," married another suitor.

Page 129. "THE BATTLE OF AGINCOURT"—*M. Drayton.* Verse 8. Line 6. *besprent*—besprinkled. The battle of Agincourt, in which a comparatively small English force under Henry V. defeated the Dauphin of France on French ground at the head of a large army, was fought on the 25th Oct. 1415. This martial lyric by the author of the Polyolbion (an elaborate descriptive and topographical poem in something like 100,000 lines,) is less known than it deserves to be. It breathes an ardent military and patriotic spirit which more than compensates for some defects of style, and which is too inadequately represented in our poetic literature. Thomas Heywood's almost forgotten play of *King Edward IV.* has the following short lyric on the same subject:

> "Agincourt, Agincourt! know ye not Agincourt?
> Where the English slew and hurt
>   All the French foemen?
> With our guns and bills brown
> Oh, the French were beat down,
>   Morris pikes and bowmen!"

Page 132. "SIR PATRICK SPENCE"—*Anonymous.* It seems to be an open question whether this poem be old or modern. The best authorities hold quite opposite opinions on the matter. Mr. Motherwell considers that it records "the fate of certain Scottish nobles who accompanied Margaret, daughter of Alexander III. of Scotland, to her nuptials with Eric king of Norway, and were drowned on their homeward voyage." This event happened A.D. 1285. Line 1. *The King sits in Dunfermline town.* There was a palace of the Scottish kings at Dunfermline, on the N. side of the Frith of Forth. Line 3. *skeely*—skilly, or skilful. L. 9. *Braid*—open, or patent. L. 13. *To Noroway*—Norway. L. 25. *hadna*—had not. L. 26. *twae*—two. L. 29. *goud*—gold. L. 30. *fee*—dowry. L. 44. *gurly*—rough. L. 45. *gude*—good. L. 54. *ane*—one. L. 59. *wap*—wrap; i. e. to stop a gap. L. 60. *letna*—let not. L. 66. *shoon*—shoes. L. 68. *aboon*—above. L. 71. *or ere*—or ever, i. e. before. L. 77. *Aberdour*—Aberdour is a little port about five miles distant from Dunfermline, now a favorite watering-place. So dangerous to mariners is all this part of the entrance to the river Forth that, according to Percy, it was called *De mortuo Mari.*

Page 135. "BURD HELEN"—*Anonymous.* "Adam Fleming, says tradition, loved Helen Irving, or Helen Bell (for this surname is uncertain, as well as the date of the occurrence) daughter of the Laird of Kirconnel in Dumfriesshire.

The lovers being together one day by the river Kirtle, a rival suitor suddenly appeared on the opposite bank, and pointed his gun; Helen threw herself before her sweetheart, received the bullet in her breast, and died in his arms. Then Adam Fleming fought with his guilty rival, and slew him."—W. Allingham. Notes to *The Book of Ballads.* Verse 2. Line 3. *burd Helen*—maiden Helen. Verse 3. L. 1. *sair*—sore. Ibid. L. 2. *mair*—more. Ibid. L. 3. *meikle*— much. Verse. 5. L. 2. *sma'*—small. Verse 9. L. 2. *een*—eyes; from *eyen.*

Page 137. "EDWARD OF THE BLOODY BRAND"—*Sir D. Dalrymple.* This striking ballad was first printed in Percy's *Reliques*, and there announced as "transmitted in MS. from Scotland by Sir D. Dalrymple, Bart, late Lord Hailes." It has been attributed to Sir D. Dalrymple, and also to Lady Wardlaw, the author of the well-known, and as Mr. W. Allingham has it, the "overpraised" ballad of Hardyknute. Verse 5. Line 4. *"dule you drie"*—grief you suffer, *Dule* is in fact *dole.*

Page 140. "ALL OR NONE"—*Sir W. Raleigh.* Verse 2. Line 1. *Angel-gold*—an Angel was an old English coin, worth about ten shillings, and of a finer quality of gold than that known as crown gold. Benedick *("Much ado about nothing"),* in his soliloquy about the sort of woman he could love, says "rich she shall be, that's certain; wise, or I'll none; virtuous, or I'll never cheapen her; fair, or I'll never look on her; mild, or come not near me; noble, or not I for an angel." This pun upon the two coins, the Noble and the Angel, seems to have escaped the observation of the commentators.

Page 162. "LOVE-SLAIN"—*W. Shakespeare.* Line 2. *sad cypress*— meaning Cyprus lawn, of which shrouds were made, and which was first manufactured in the Isle of Cyprus.

Page 163. "INCONSTANCY"—*W. Shakespeare.* Shakespeare's claim to these stanzas is somewhat doubtful. The first only appears in *"Measure for Measure,"* while both are found in Beaumont and Fletcher's *'Rollo, Duke of Normandy.'* On the other hand, both verses are attributed to Shakespeare in the 1640 Edition of his poems.

Page 167. "MAD-SONG"—*W. Blake.* Verse 1. Line 7. *Rustling beds of dawn*—Mr. Gilchrist prints this "rustling *birds* of dawn." Mr. Rossetti has it "beds," as Blake printed it.

Page 168. "ARIEL'S SONG"—*W. Shakespeare.* Line 5. *after sunset*— Theobald reads *sunset,* because the bat does not come out before twilight, and this is the version adopted by Dr. Arne. Most editors adhere to "Summer" as printed in the first Folio of 1623.

Page 168. "A FAIRY'S SONG"—Ibid. Line 8. *Her orbs*—the rings dried up on the sward, where the fairies have been dancing in circles. See an allusion to the same superstition in the two last lines of the next following poem.

Page 169. "THE FAIRY QUEEN"—*Anonymous.* Verse 3. Line 4. *manchet*—a small loaf of fine white bread.

Page 171. "SONG OF AN ENCHANTRESS"—*Giles Fletcher.* This beautiful song, which has in it not only a ring of Spenser's music, but a distant echo of Ariosto, is from that almost forgotten but very remarkable poem "The Purple Island."

Page 173. "A VISION OF 'THE FAERY QUEEN'"—*Sir W. Raleigh*. Line 12. *perse*—pierce. L. 13. *sprighte*—spirit. Leigh Hunt says—"Two persons, I have no doubt, were included in the magnificent flattery of this sonnet—Queen Elizabeth as well as Spenser; for it was she whom the poet expressly imaged in his Queen of Fairyland; and Sir W. Raleigh was not the man to let the occasion pass for extolling that great woman, their joint mistress. His abolition of Laura, Petrarch, and Homer all in a lump, in honour of his friend Spenser is in the highest style of his wilful and somewhat domineering genius: but everything in the poem is as grandly as it is summarily done."

Page 175. "To HIS LOVE"—*W. Shakespeare*. This sonnet is introduced here in the above connection, inasmuch as it evidently conveys a complimentary allusion to Spenser.

Page 179. "TRUTH THE SOUL OF BEAUTY"—Ibid. Line 9. *But for their virtue only is their show*, another inversion, as in the last line of Sir P. Sidney's sonnet to the Moon. It means—"but that their show only is their virtue."

Page 180. "THE PAINS OF MEMORY"—*W. Drummond.* One of the richest and tenderest of Elizabethan sonnets. The Alexis to whom it is addressed was probably the poet's friend William Alexander, Earl of Stirling. Line 14. *sith*—since.

Page 182. "To MR. LAWRENCE"—*J. Milton*. This Mr. Lawrence was the son of the President of Cromwell's Council. Line 6. *Favonius*—the spring wind. This sonnet, a model of neat and elegant classicism, might have been written by Horace to Mæcenas.

Page 203. "A RURAL PICTURE"—*O. Goldsmith.* To give complete poems and eschew extracts, has been a leading principle of construction throughout this volume. In the present instance, however, the Editor feels that some apology is due for the liberty taken in cutting and adapting certain passages from the "Deserted Village." Not a word, however, has been altered, and the extract thus arranged presents, it is believed, a fair representative specimen of Goldsmith's manner.

Page 205. "ODE TO EVENING"—*W. Collins*. Verse 2. Line 3. *Brede ethereal*—braid; used by Keats in the sense of chain, or procession. See *Ode to a Grecian Urn*—"with *brede* of marble men and maidens overwrought."

Page 207. "ELEGY WRITTEN IN A COUNTRY CHURCHYARD"—*T. Gray.* "Had Gray written nothing but his Elegy, high as he stands, I am not sure that he would not stand higher. It is the corner-stone of his glory."—*Lord Byron*. "Perhaps the noblest stanzas in our language"—*F. T. Palgrave*.

Page 213. "THE BIRKS OF INVERMAY"—*D. Mallet. Birks*—i. e. birches.

Page 215. "THE BIRD"—*H. Vaughan*. A most tender and touching picture of the life of a bird; at once the most innocent and spiritual of created existences.

Page 217. "THE TIGER"—*W. Blake*. There are two versions of this noble poem. The one here given is that printed by Blake in his *Songs of Experience*. The other, containing some unimportant variations from a MS. authority, may be found in Gilchrist's '*Life of Blake*.'

Page 229. "Cupid's Mistake"—*M. Prior*. This poem and the one by which it is followed, are given, not for their poetical merit, which is slender, but as specimens of the *vers d'occasion* of the time, and as necessary links in the chain of English verse.

Page 230. "Love's Patience." Verse 5. Line 4. *ure*—custom, habit used here to signify that spring follows winter according to custom.

Page 232. "Love's Might"—*Beaumont and Fletcher*. From a play by Beaumont and Fletcher called *The Little French Lawyer*. To assign the exact authorship of this delightful lyric would not be easy. Leigh Hunt especially admired the third line of the 2d verse—*Fear the fierceness of the boy*—than which, he writes, "nothing can be finer. Wonder and earnestness conspire to stamp the iteration of the sound." Vide *Imagination and Fancy*.

Page 235. "Love's Prisoner"—*W. Blake*. "This lovely lyric is affirmed to have been written by Blake before he was fourteen years of age."—W. M. Rossetti. Notes to *The Poetical Works of W. Blake*.

Page 236. "To Nancy"—*Bishop Percy of Dromore*. Robert Burns pronounced this song to be the most beautiful composition of its kind in the English language.

Page 237. "Sally in our Alley"—*Henry Carey*. "A little masterpiece in a very difficult style. Catullus himself could hardly have bettered it. In grace, tenderness, simplicity and humour, it is worthy of the Ancients; and even more so, from the completeness and unity of the picture presented." W. G. Palgrave. Notes to *The Golden Treasury*. H. Carey was a musician and song-writer, and author of some minor dramatic works, published in 1743. He wrote, among other things, a farce called *Hanging and Marriage*, and some *Verses on Gulliver's Travels*.

Page 241. "Ye Gentlemen of England"—*Martyn Parker*. It is said of Campbell that he used frequently to repeat this poem, and that he warmly admired it. It undoubtedly suggested to him that noblest of sea-songs, *Ye Mariners of England*.

Page 242. "To all you Ladies now on Land"—*Lord Dorset*. In 1665, Lord Buckhurst, afterwards Earl of Dorset, attended the Duke of York as a volunteer in the Dutch war, and was in the battle of June 3d when eighteen Dutch ships were taken, fourteen others destroyed, and Opdam the Admiral, who engaged the Duke, was blown up beside him, with all his crew. On the day before the battle, he is said to have composed the celebrated song *To all you Ladies now on Land*, with equal tranquillity of mind and promptitude of wit. Seldom any splendid story is wholly true. "I have heard from the late Earl of Orrery, who was likely to have had good hereditary intelligence, that Lord Buckhurst had been a week employed upon it, and only retouched or finished it on the memorable evening. But even this, whatever it may subtract from his facility, leaves him his courage." Dr. Johnson.

Page 245. "The Loss of the Royal George"—*W. Cowper*. The Royal George, of 108 guns, whilst undergoing a partial careening in Portsmouth Harbour, was overset about 10 A.M. Aug. 29, 1782. The total loss was believed to be near 1000 souls.

Page 247. "A Dirge"—*T. Chatterton*. Verse 2. Line 1. *cryne*—hair. Ibid. L. 2. *Rode*—complexion. Verse 6. L. 4. *calness*—coldness. Verse 7. L. 1. *dent*—fix. Ibid. L. 2. *gree*—grew. Ibid. L. 3. *ouphant*—elfin. Verse 9. L. 1. *reytes*—water-flags.

Page 249. "Yarrow Stream"—*J. Logan*. Founded on an old Scottish legend, also versified anonymously in a ballad called "Willy drowned in Yarrow." See *Golden Treasury*, Book III. No. CXXVIII.

Page 251. "Bonnie George Campbell"—*Anonymous*. This ballad is founded on a common incident of border life in the wild days of old.

Page 252. "Love's Lamentation"—*Anonymous*. Line 1. *O Waly, waly*—a cry of lamentation; see *King Lear*, Act IV. Sc. 6. : "the first time that we smell the ayre, we *wawle* and cry" Ed. 1623. Verse 1. L. 2. *Brae*—hillside. Ibid. L. 3. *burn-side*—brook-side. Verse 2. L. 5. *busk*—in the sense of array, or adorn. Verse 3. L. 3. *Saint Anton's well*—a spring at the foot of Arthur's Seat. ·Verse 4. L. 8. *cramasie*—from the French *cramoisie*—crimson. "A very ancient song."—Bishop Percy.

Page 253. "Auld Robin Gray"—*Lady A. Barnard*. "There can hardly exist a poem more truly tragic in the highest sense than this; nor, except Sappho, has any poet known to the Editor equalled it in excellence." W. G. Palgrave. Notes to *The Golden Treasury*. Lady A. Barnard was the daughter of James Lindsay, 5th Earl of Balcarras, and wife of Sir Andrew Barnard, librarian to George III. Having kept the authorship of this celebrated ballad strictly secret for more than fifty years, Lady Anne Barnard acknowledged it for her own in a letter to Sir W. Scott in A.D. 1823. The story of the ballad was altogether a fiction. Robin Gray was her father's gardener, and no such persons as Jamie or the heroine ever existed, save in the imagination of the Lady Anne.

Page 255. "To Mary Unwin"—*W. Cowper*. The Mary Unwin of these purely pathetic and tragic lines, was the faithful friend whose solicitude soothed, while she lived, the clouded and declining years of the poet's unhappy life.

Page 258. "Alexander's Feast"—*J. Dryden*. Line 1. *'Twas at the royal feast*—Alexander is recorded to have held a great banquet on the occasion of his victory at Persepolis, and to have set fire to the palace in his mad revelry. An Athenian courtesan named Thais is said to have instigated him to the act. Timotheus was a famous flute-player of Thebes; but Dryden makes him a performer on the lyre. His music is said to have been so soul-stirring that the King is reputed to have started up and seized his arms on one occasion when Timotheus was performing an Orthian nome to Athena. L. 46. *drinking is the soldier's pleasure*—a fragment of Menander quoted by Athenæus describes the drunkenness of Alexander as proverbial. L. 130. *divine Cecilia*—Saint Cecilia, a Roman lady of the 3d Century, who is said to have excelled so surpassingly in music that an angel was attracted down from heaven by the charms of her voice. It is a mistake to attribute the invention of the organ to St. Cecilia (who is nevertheless the patron saint of music and musicians); that honour belonging traditionally to Archimedes, about 220. B.C.

Page 262. "Ode on St. Cecilia's Day"—*A. Pope*. Line 39. *The*

Thracian—Orpheus, who accompanied Jason when he departed in quest of the Golden Fleece. L. 40. *Argo*—the galley of Jason, the wood of which, according to Pope, recognised, and thrilled responsively towards, the trees that came down the mountain side to the sound of Orpheus' lyre; one of the most beautiful figures in the whole of Pope's poetry. L. 50. *Phlegethon*—a fiery river of the lower world. L. 99. *Hebrus*—see note to Lycidas. L. 109. *Rhodope*— a range of mountains in Thrace. L. 111. *Hæmus*—another mountain-range in Thrace. L. 133. *His numbers rais'd a shade*—the epigrammatic antithesis is curiously imitative of that which concludes the preceding poem.

 Page 267. "ODE ON THE UNIVERSE"—*J. Addison.* The great essayist's strongest claim to a place among the British poets rests upon this noble ode, which for simple majesty, and breadth of both style and feeling, is unrivalled.

 Page 268. "ODE ON THE MORNING OF CHRIST'S NATIVITY"—*John Milton.* Verse 4. Line 4. *The hookéd chariot*—Chariots armed with scythes and hooks were in use as engines of war in ancient Syria and Persia, and, according to Cæsar, were a formidable weapon of the ancient Britons. Verse 5. L. 4. *whist*—silenced. Todd quotes, in illustration of this passage, the following line from Marlowe and Nash's *Dido* (1594.)

   " The ayre is cleere and Southerne windes are whist"

Verse 8. L. 5. Milton here uses the name of Pan, the Hellenic God of the Universe, in the sense of Christ, the Lord of All. Dante, no less daringly, addresses Christ as *sommo Giove*, high Jove. Verse 10. L. 3. *Cynthia*—the moon. Verse 13. L. 7. *ninefold harmony*—the harmony of the spheres, which Milton elsewhere describes as "nine-enfolded." Verse 20. L. 3. *A voice of weeping heard and loud lament*—Plutarch tells of a mighty voice that was heard in the air proclaiming "Great Pan is dead!" whereupon the oracles ceased, and there was universal lamentation. This story, as told by the early Christian commentators, is made to date from the hour of Christ's Nativity. Verse 21. L. 3. *The Lars and Lemurés*—the household Gods of the Romans. Ibid. L. 6. *Affrights the Flamens at their service quaint*—Flamen was a sacerdotal title pertaining to any Roman priest who was devoted to the service of one especial God. *Quaint* is probably here used in the sense of curious, or perhaps of fantastic. It has lately been suggested by a correspondent of *The Academy* that the word employed by Milton was *quent*, an early form of *quenched*. Verse 22. L. 1. *Baalim* is here used in the sense of Gods only; the true meaning of the word being the lesser Baals, or local minor Gods, who were emanations of Baal, the great God of the Phœnicians. Baal-Peor was one of these, and has by some commentators been identified with Priapus. Ibid. L. 3. *twice-battered God of Palestine*—Dagon. Ibid. L. 4. *Moonéd Ashtoroth*—Astarte, the local Goddess of Sidon, identified later with the Greek Aphrodite. Astarte was one of those Phœnician deities who were admitted into the Egyptian pantheon. She is represented at Edfoo in Upper Egypt with the head of a lioness, and crowned with the solar disk. Milton had evidently seen some representation of Astarte crowned in this manner, and had mistaken the disk for that of the moon. Ibid. L. 7. *Lybic Hammon shrinks his horn*—an allusion to the Egyptian Amen, the deity worshipped at the Oasis of Amen, now called the oasis of El Khargeh, which lies W. of the

Nile in N. Lat. 26°, and where there are considerable ruins. This deity, commonly called Jupiter Ammon, was in a measure identified with Kneph, the ram-headed and demiurgic type of the supreme Amen, and was represented horned. An inscription of the elder Darius still extant on the walls of the temple at El Khargeh says "thy horns are pointed, twisted are thy horns;" and describes the God as "horned in all his beauty." The fossils called Ammonites derive their name, curiously enough, from a fancied resemblance to the horns of this God. Ibid. L. 8. *their wounded Thammuz*—a Syrian mythological hero, son of a Syrian King, and beloved by Astarte (see preceding note). He was fabled as dying of a wound received from a wild boar, and as reviving for the six months of spring and summer in each year. Thammuz is better known as Adonis, under which name he came eventually to be worshipped in nearly all countries bordering upon the Mediterranean. The cult of Thammuz is in fact the worship of the revival of nature in spring and summer, and is of purely Phœnician origin. Verse 23. L. 1. *Sullen Moloch*— a brazen idol fashioned in the form of a man with the head of a calf, worshipped with sacrifices of living children by the Hebrews in the valley of Tophet. Verse 23. L. 8. *Isis and Orus and the dog Anubis* – Isis, the wife and sister of Osiris, is represented crowned with the sun-disk and horns, and is sometimes figured under the form of a cow. She was the mother of Horus, whose name Milton has spelt without the H. Horus is usually represented in the form of a hawk. Anubis was the God who presided over the offices of embalming and the rites of sepulture. He is represented with the head not of a dog, but a jackal. Verse 24. L. 1. *Osiris* – the God of the lower world, and judge of the dead. Mr. Palgrave says: "Osiris, the Egyptian God of Agriculture (here, perhaps by confusion with Apis, figured as a Bull), was torn to pieces by Typho and embalmed after death in a sacred chest."—See Notes to Page 47, Book II. *Golden Treasury*. This definition, however, is not altogether satisfactory. Osiris, in so far as he is identified with Dionysus, the friend, benefactor, and instructor of man, may certainly be described as the Egyptian God of Agriculture; but he is primarily and principally the Deity of the Lower World, the Judge of the Dead, the Great Spirit of the life to come, to whom the justified dead are re-united, and in whose essence they are absorbed. Apis could scarcely, from any point of view, be "confused" with Osiris. The bull Apis was, in fact, Osiris in the flesh. In other words, he was the outward and visible manifestation of Osiris upon earth; the temporary, but chosen, dwelling of the divinity. Philosophically defined, Osiris is the nocturnal sun; i. e. the sun below the horizon; he who dies each evening, descends into the shades, and rises again at morn. He plays in fact the chief part in the great Solar myth which underlies the whole religious system of ancient Egypt. Ibid. L. 2. *Memphian grove* – Every Egyptian Temple had its temenos, or consecrated enclosure, within which was planted the sacred grove. Ibid. L. 3. *the unshowered grass* – an allusion to the dryness of the Egyptian climate. It is a mistake, however, to suppose that it does not rain in Lower and Middle Egypt. Showers are frequent in the Delta, and by no means rare at Cairo. It is probable, indeed, that when Memphis was a great city surrounded by gardens, groves, and cultivated lands, rain may have fallen even more frequently than now.   Ibid. L. 8. *The sable stoléd sorcerers bear his worshipt ark—* These sable stoled priests are a picturesque device of the poet.   The monumental evidence all goes to show that the priesthood were clothed in white robes, over which, when engaged in the celebration of high religious ceremonies, they wore a panther skin upon the shoulders.   The sacred ark was made in the form of a boat and adorned with a central shrine supported by winged genii.   This shrine, which contained the image, or symbol, of the God, was covered by a veil; and the boat was generally decorated at prow and stern with carved rams' heads, emblematic of Kneph the creative, or primal deity. This ark was carried on men's shoulders by means of poles and rings.   See the Mosaic description of the ark of the Covenant, which was unquestionably modelled on the sacred arks of the Egyptians.   Verse 25. L. 6. *Typhon huge ending in snaky twine.*—The Typhon of the Egyptians was usually represented under the form of an animal resembling an ass, with pointed ears and a long sharp muzzle.   In later times—that is, during the period of Roman rule—he appears as a dragon, and Horus, who slew him, takes the form of a hawk-headed warrior in Roman costume.   In these representations, M. Clermont Ganneau has recognised the origin of the myth of St. George and the Dragon. St. George, it should be added, is the patron saint of the Coptic Christians, as Horus was the favorite warrior-deity of their pagan forefathers.   Here, then, as in so many other instances, we see conversion made easy by the translation of a local God into a Christian saint.   The Etruscan Typhon is represented as a man to the waist, with twisted snakes for legs.   Milton had probably seen some antique Etruscan gem engraved with this type.   Verse 27. L. 8. *bright harnesd angels*—i. e. bright-armoured.   In old French, *harnois* was man's armour, *harnais* was horse's armour; which latter, with an altered application, survives as *harness* in the English of to-day.

CHRONOLOGICAL TABLE OF AUTHORS.

	Born	Died
Chaucer, Geoffrey	1328	1400
James I. (of Scotland)	1394	1437
Skelton, John	1460	1529
Wyatt, Thomas	1503	1542
Howard, Henry (Earl of Surrey)	1515	1547
Raleigh, Sir Walter	1552	1618
Spenser, Edmund	1553	1599
Lylye, John	1553	1601
Sidney, Sir Philip	1554	1586
Greville, Fulke, (Lord Brooke)	1554	1628
Lodge, Thomas	1556	1625
Greene, Robert	1560	1592
Southwell, Robert	1560	1595
Bacon, Francis (Lord)	1561	1626
Harrington, Sir John	1561	1612
Sylvestre, Joshua	1563	1618
Drayton, Michael	1563	1631
Marlowe, Christopher	1564	1593
Shakespeare, William	1564	1616

	Born	Died
Nash, Thomas	1567	1600
Wotton, Sir Henry	1568	1639
Donne, Dr. John	1573	1631
Jonson, Ben	1574	1637
Fletcher, John	1576	1625
Burton, Robert	1576	1640
Dekker, Thomas	?	1641
Rowley, Samuel	(XVIth Century)	
Barnefield, Richard	(XVIth Century)	
Webster, John	(XVIth Century)	
Drummond, William	1585	1649
Beaumont, Francis	1586	1616
Ford, John	1586	1639
Kinaston, Sir Francis	1587	1642(?)
Fletcher, Giles	1588	1623
Wither, George	1588	1667
Carew, Thomas	1589	1639
Browne, William	1590	1645
Herrick, Robert	1591	1674
King, Dr. Henry	1591	1669
Herbert, George	1593	1632
Shirley, James	1594	1666
Strode, William	1600	1644
Parker, Martyn	(XVIIth Century)	
Wastell, Simon	(XVIIth Century)	
Davenant, Sir William	1605	1668
Habington, William	1605	1645
Waller, Edmund	1605	1687
Heywood, Thomas	1607	1649(?)
Milton, John	1608	1674
Suckling, Sir John	1609	1641
Feltham, Owen	1610	1673

	Born	Died
Cartwright, William	1611	1643
Grahame, James (Marquis of Montrose)	1612	1650
Crashaw, Richard	1615	1652
Cowley, Abraham	1618	1667
Lovelace, Colonel Richard	1618	1658
Marvell, Andrew	1620	1678
Vaughan, Henry	1621	1695
Stanley, Thomas	1625	1678
Dryden, John	1631	1700
Sackville, Charles (Earl of Dorset)	1637	1706
Sedley, Sir Charles	1639	1701
Prior, Matthew	1664	1721
Sewell, George	?	1726
Hamilton, Charles (Lord Binney)	?	1732
Swift, Jonathan	1667	1745
Addison, Joseph	1672	1719
Carey, Henry	?	1743
Pope, Alexander	1688	1744
Gay, John	1688	1732
Thomson, James	1700	1748
Mallet, David	1700	1765
Lyttleton, George (Lord)	1709	1773
Shenstone, William	1714	1763
Gray, Thomas	1716	1771
Collins, William	1720	1756
Smollett, Tobias	1721	1771
Dalrymple, Sir David (Lord Hailes)	1726	1792
Goldsmith, Oliver	1728	1774
Elliot, Sir Gilbert	?	1777
Percy, Thomas (Bishop of Dromore)	1728	1811
Cowper, William	1731	1800
Beattie, John	1735	1803

	Born	Died
Logan, John	1748 .	1788
Barnard, Lady Anne	1750 .	1825
Chatterton, Thomas	1752 .	1770
Blake, William	1757 .	1827

PRINTING OFFICE OF THE PUBLISHER.